# FRAGILE BONES
## HARRISON AND ANNA

Text copyright © 2015 by Lorna Schultz Nicholson

Published by Clockwise Press Inc., 201 Taylor Mills Drive
North, Richmond Hill, Ontario, L4C 2T5

www.clockwisepress.com

christie@clockwisepress.com    solange@clockwisepress.com

10 9 8 7 6 5 4 3 2 1

Library and Archives Canada Cataloguing in Publication

Fragile Bones: Harrison & Anna (A One-2-One Book)
ISBN 978-0-99393-510-7 (Paperback)
Data available on file

Publisher Cataloging-in-Publication Data (U.S.)
Fragile Bones: Harrison and Anna (A One-2-One Book)
ISBN 978-0-99393-510-7 (Paperback)
Data available on file

Cover Design by Tanya Montini
Interior design by CommTech Unlimited
Printed in Canada by Webcom

# FRAGILE BONES
## HARRISON AND ANNA

## A ONE-2-ONE BOOK

*Lorna Schultz Nicholson*

CLOCKWISE
PRESS

# AUTHOR'S NOTE

The Best Buddies is a real program that operates in schools, including colleges, all over the world. Students with intellectual disabilities pair up with volunteer peer "Buddies." They meet together, one-to-one, at least twice monthly to engage in fun, social interaction. They also participate in group activities. That said, this is a work of fiction. Harrison and Anna are fictional characters and I made them up. I also made up where they live, their high school, their families and all their situations, like the Halloween dance. Yes, I did a tremendous amount of research so I could write the novel but in the end it is a work of fiction. Fiction is pleasure reading. So, please, enjoy!

# TO DIVERSITY:

Every child deserves respect, compassion,
and a chance to succeed.

# TO DIVERSITY:

Every child deserves respect, compassion,
and a chance to succeed.

# CHAPTER ONE
## HARRISON

Round the corner. Three steps. Round the corner. Three steps.

"Stop walking in those circles." My brother spoke but I didn't listen.

The sounds from the school hallway were swirling, spinning in my head: laughter, talking, feet on the tiles, humming, words, lots of words, including Joel talking to me. Around the corner. Three steps. I couldn't stop walking in circles, I just couldn't. Right now it was helping me process what was getting trapped inside my head. Everything was spinning and if it spun too much, it would make me explode.

"Just stop," said Joel. "You're going to be fine."

Round the corner. Three steps. Round the corner. Three steps.

This meeting wasn't what I usually did on Tuesdays. On Tuesdays after school I waited for Joel at the front entrance of the high school I attended by the big Canadian flag, which hung from the wall in a little holster. I had done the same thing every Tuesday since I started attending Sir Winston Churchill Secondary School, which was twenty-one days ago. I had math last period, then I waited for my older brother, Joel. On Tuesdays I wore a white t-shirt and tan-coloured pants and boxers underneath my pants, always boxers, so I didn't flush my underwear down the toilet. Boxers without the tags don't scratch me. My mom puts a soft covering over all my tags, especially my underwear tags, and I haven't blocked a school toilet in 784 days. And Joel always meets me at the flag and drives me home and I'm always home by 3:30 to watch *Grey's Anatomy*.

"There are 206 bones in the body," I said. "The arm has three main bones. Humerus, ulna, and radius." I looked at the floor. Three steps. Round the corner.

"Please, don't start with the bones," said Joel. "And stop walking in circles. Mom said you have to go to this meeting. That I had to make you go."

"Ten wrist bones. Scaphoid, lunate, triquetral —"

"Harrison!" Joel spoke in a louder voice. I heard him breathing.

"Breathe, Bud, okay?" he said. This time his voice was softer. He'd had to go to the doctor too to learn how to control his voice and his yelling by breathing. Mom didn't like it when he yelled at me, which wasn't that often, but when we were little if I broke one of his toys he yelled, and now he yelled if I interrupted him and his girlfriend when they were kissing on the sofa. I don't like it when he kisses on the sofa because viruses and bacterial infections are transmitted through saliva.

"Breathe, Harrison," he said. "In through the nose, count to three, and out through the mouth for a count of three. In and out."

I took in a big breath of air and let it out. Was today going to be a good day or a bad day? The noises and words were like one of those rides that went round and round at the park, one that I couldn't get off. I had to breathe. Joel told me to breathe. I knew I should also tell my legs to stop.

"Stop," I said. "Stop. Stop." I could only say it three times because I liked the number three. The number seven made me sick but I liked eight. It was my favourite number. I breathed in and out.

My brain slowed, the spinning lessened a little. The breathing *was* helping the spinning. And talking to my legs was helping me to stop walking in circles.

"Okay," said Joel, "that's better. Now, walk into that room and sit down. I'm going to wait for you."

"You'll wait outside this door?"

"Yes. Right outside the door."

"You'll wait for sure?"

"Yes. Go in the room and sit on your hands if you have to."

I stood outside the door. "Pisiform, trapezium, trapezoid, capitate, and hamate."

"This will be good for you," said Joel. "And good for me too." He said that in a quieter voice, which my mother would say was "under his breath" but to me that made no sense because words can't possibly be under someone's breath. The voice is a sound and doesn't have a physical structure so something can't be *underneath* it.

"Hey, Joel." I heard a girl's voice.

I shook my head. "I'm missing *Grey's Anatomy*."

"They're reruns. Mom taped it anyway."

"I'm supposed to watch it at 3:30."

"Today you'll watch it at 4:30. Come on, you have to do

9

this." He paused. "Hey, Beth, how's it going?"

I didn't want to look but I did. Joel had a girl standing beside him and this was normal for him because he always has lots of girls by his side. Sometimes, when my parents are out and we are at home by ourselves, a girl will ring the doorbell and come into the house. He will kiss the girl and the latest girl is Amy and not Beth, the girl standing beside him right now. One time when I was home alone with Joel, Amy came over and they kissed a lot. When my mom came home I asked her if Joel could get AIDS from kissing. Joel got mad at me because Mom got mad at Joel for letting the girl in the house and maybe it was because she knew it was bad for Joel to be kissing. If the girl had an open sore on her mouth he could get herpes or hepatitis B. Was he going to kiss Beth in the hallway? I wouldn't want that to happen because I was too close to them and I might actually see the saliva being exchanged. I knew I wouldn't be able to handle that, especially today when I had to go to a meeting with people I didn't know and couldn't go home to watch *Grey's Anatomy*.

"Mom will be mad at *me* if you don't go in." Joel pointed in the room. "See that desk by the door? Go sit down there. I promise I will watch you from here. And when they close the door I will stay right here in this spot. Just sit on those big mitts of yours."

The girl laughed. "Look at this," she said.

I looked at my hands. "I'm not wearing mittens," I said. "I don't wear them until it snows."

"I meant hands," said Joel while looking at the girl's phone.

The girl laughed again and her voice was high and

sometimes girls laughed at me like that when I did something they thought was 'stupid.'

"She's laughing," I said.

"Not at you," Joel replied. "At a text." He held up her phone and showed me but I didn't care to see the text. Reading other people's texts or emails is inappropriate. I do a lot of things that are inappropriate or at least that's what my parents are always saying and the psychologists too.

"Oh," I said. Joel and this Beth girl went back to reading texts on her phone and laughing. I'd never laughed with a girl before. I turned and looked into the room and saw the empty desk Joel had pointed to and it was close to the door. I had to do this. My mom said I had to go to this meeting. This kind of thing was "good for me."

I stepped over the line separating the hall and the door. Then I brought my foot back. I had to test the line first. Going into a new room made me anxious. Step. Tap. Back. Step. Tap. Back. Breathe. Step forward. Over. In.

On the third try I was in. Always on the third try.

As soon as I knew I was in, I glanced at the floor and moved as quickly as I could to the desk Joel had pointed out for me. I slid into the seat and stared at the desk top. Someone had written all over the top of the desk.

I pulled out some sanitary wipes from my backpack and rubbed them across the desk.

A low voice started talking from the front of the room. I kept wiping.

"Welcome to Best Buddies," said the voice of a boy I didn't know. "My name is Justin and I'm the Chapter President of the Best Buddies program for our high school. It's awesome that you've all shown up today."

I wiped harder. And harder. I knew I should stop. "Sit on your hands," I whispered. "Sit on your hands."

I sat on my hands. Palms down. There are ten wrist bones.

"From the form you filled out online, about your interests and such," continued Justin, "we will pair you up. Mrs. Beddington is going to help with that job."

I know Mrs. Beddington. She is my guidance counsellor and I like her because she takes the time to understand me and listens to what I have to say, and she never lets the other kids say mean things to me or tell me what I'm saying is stupid. She thinks what I say is intelligent and I appreciate that, and she listens when I talk about the human body and all its bones and muscles and systems and when I talk about diseases and how they are transmitted.

I glanced up and saw her sitting at the front of the room, on a chair, not a desk, with her legs crossed at the ankle, wearing low sensible shoes, and smiling as usual. She always smiles and she has perfect white teeth that look like fluorescent lights. She also has high cheekbones. There are fourteen facial bones.

"Once you have your partner, you will get in touch with each other and make meeting dates, which can be as simple as going for a walk or for coffee. You don't have to spend a lot of money; just do something together. After all, most of us kids don't have a lot of cash."

A few people laughed. I didn't because I didn't think it was funny because it was a fact. And I didn't want to go for coffee because I don't like coffee.

"We are also going to be planning three events for the year. One will be a dance that will take place after school and I think it will be a Halloween dance."

The word *dance* made its way into my brain and I could feel it leaching, sticking to the side wall. On television shows, students in high school went to dances and Joel went to the dances. Last year he'd gotten all dressed up in a suit to go to a dance and he'd bought the girl he was taking as his date a flower to put on her wrist. I'm not sure why it is called a date when a date is something that grows on a palm tree, and his date wasn't Beth who was in the hall with him, but Amy.

Justin kept talking. "I'm open to suggestions for that event and for ideas for the other two events. Maybe we can do a games night or something like that. I'd like to form a few committees to work on the events so if you're interested I've got a few sheets here so you can sign up."

Justin was holding up papers, and I was still sitting on my hands and that was a good thing and I had looked at him, once, which was also a good thing. I didn't want to look at Justin for too long though because then he might see this and try to make eye contact with me so I stared at the floor and everyone's shoes. The psychologist and my parents said that every day I was supposed to look one person in the eyes. When I asked if that was a rule they said not really but if I wanted to make it a rule that was okay, which didn't make sense because why would I *make* something a rule when it wasn't? I didn't understand why I had to try if it made me uncomfortable. It was like wearing underwear or shirts with tags.

The first pair of shoes I saw were running shoes and I liked that because most running shoes had good arch support and weren't hard on the bones of the feet. Another person wore pink flat shoes with the name *Tom's* on the heel and I wondered why a boy would wear pink shoes so I quickly glanced up to see that it wasn't a boy but a girl who must have had a boy's name. Then I saw another pair of running shoes and another pair of running shoes.

And high heels.

I turned my gaze back to the desk top. High heels are hard on the bones of the feet because they put the feet in an unnatural position and cause stress to bones in the foot arches. My mom doesn't wear them. The last time she wore them I had a meltdown because my mind started spinning with how she was going to hurt her feet. There are twenty-six bones in each foot.

"Are there any questions?" Justin asked.

A girl sitting across the room from me asked, "When can we find out who our Buddy is?"

My hands underneath my thighs wanted to flap so I pressed my thighs against them. "Sit on your hands," I said. "Sit on your hands." I was going to have a Buddy from *this* room. I kept staring at the top of the desk because what if my Buddy ended up being the person who was wearing the high heels? What if that same person wore perfume or cologne? Or liked the number seven? What if it was a girl and she wanted me to kiss her, and I got mononucleosis or herpes or even hepatitis B from kissing her because we shared saliva or she had an open sore that I couldn't detect with the naked eye?

"As early as tomorrow morning." This time it was Mrs. Beddington who spoke. I relaxed a little because I knew she liked me and wouldn't get mad at me for talking to myself. She continued and said, "I will be in my office all day so just pop by to see me and I will give out all the information."

There was another question and another question.

"There are twenty bones in the hand," I whispered, continuing to sit harder and harder on my hands until they hurt.

The total number of questions was eight and that was a good thing because eight is my favourite number. When the room became silent and there were no more questions, Justin said, "Well, if that's all the questions, this meeting is adjourned. Remember, sign-up sheets are at the front, and contact Mrs. Beddington tomorrow to find out who your Best Buddy is."

As soon as I heard the scraping of desks on the floor, I bolted for the door. Joel was waiting for me outside the door, like he said.

"You ready?" he asked.

I nodded.

We walked to the car without talking. When I got in the front seat he looked at me. "Really?"

"Mom said I had to if the parking lot was empty," I replied, putting on my seat belt. "The odds of you hitting another car, or another car hitting you, are drastically reduced just from the car-versus-car ratio in the parking lot."

"Whatever," said Joel.

We weren't even out of the parking lot when he said, "There were a lot of cute girls coming out of that meeting. Maybe you'll hook up with one and have a girlfriend."

"I don't want a girlfriend. I don't want to kiss someone on the lips because I don't want to get a virus or bacterial infection. There's a stop sign coming up," I said. "In forty-three metres."

Joel braked at the stop sign and I lurched into the dashboard. "You need to press the brakes *before* you reach the sign," I said.

"I'm the one driving," he replied. "I did pass my driver's test." He started driving again and I glanced over at the speedometer.

"You're exceeding the speed limit."

"One day you're going to have to at least hold hands with a girl with or without hand sanitizer." He turned on the radio to some rock music station and sat back in his seat, putting his one arm out his window.

I turned the radio off and said, "You need to concentrate on your driving." I pointed out the window at the road stretching in front of us, a road I was familiar with because we drove it every morning and every night. I didn't like short cuts so Joel and my mom and dad drove the same way to school when I was in the car.

"Over 10% of all drivers under the age of 20 who are involved in fatal crashes were reported as distracted at the time of the crash," I said. "Your age has the largest proportion of distracted drivers."

"Music isn't considered distracting." Joel turned the radio back on.

"You should put two hands on the wheel. Having one hand on the wheel is being distracted. There is another stop sign in 153 metres."

"Why did you insist on sitting in the front seat?"

"The odds of us being in an accident in the parking lot were reduced because the number of cars had been reduced." I pointed out the window. "The stop sign is coming up and because you are driving five kilometres over the speed limit you should begin braking now."

Joel cranked the wheel and pulled over to the side of

the road. He opened the glove compartment and pulled out a hand-held video game. "Get in the back," he said, "and play your video game."

I unsnapped my seat belt, opened my car door, and stepped onto the shoulder of the road. After a car whizzed by our car, I quickly got into the back. Once my door was shut and my seat belt done up, Joel turned around to look at me. "Don't watch the road," he said.

Slouching in my seat, I turned on *First Responders*, my favourite video game where I got to be the paramedic on the scene and learn about all the injuries and how they were going to fix them. I was on my third accident when Joel pulled into our driveway.

He got out of the car without saying anything to me and slammed his door. As soon as I walked into the mud room, which was off our garage, my mother came out from the kitchen, wiping her hands on a dish cloth. "How did it go?" she asked.

Joel slipped out of his shoes, leaving them to just sit on the floor in a pile and walked right by Mom. I took my shoes off and put them in the cubby that had my name on it.

"Harrison?" She said my name like a question.

"Did you record *Grey's Anatomy*?" I asked.

"Of course I did," she replied. "Can you answer my question?"

"I can't answer a question when you just said my name."

"Before I said your name, I asked you how the meeting went," she said.

"I sat on my hands and didn't look at anyone but I did look at their feet and most of them were wearing running shoes or flat shoes except there was one girl and she was wearing high heels and Mrs. Beddington was there."

"O-kay. Do you know when you get your Buddy?"

"Tomorrow."

"Oh, that's good."

"What if it's the girl who wears the high heels? High heels are bad for the feet and they put stress on the bones. They said we might have to go for coffee and I don't want to go for coffee because I don't like coffee. What if I get a girl and she wants me to hold her hand? And she sweats and I get a virus or some sort of bacteria that can be transmitted through sweat? Or she wants me to kiss her and she has an open sore and I get herpes or hepatitis B?"

"You've been vaccinated for hepatitis B. I told you that already."

"I haven't been vaccinated for mononucleosis, which is a form of glandular fever and is transmitted through saliva."

"Harrison, are you spinning?"

# CHAPTER TWO
## ANNA

The balled up piece of paper hit me on the side of the head, making me turn. My best friend, Marnie, sitting in the desk kitty-corner to me, was grinning and holding up her phone, miming that she'd sent me a text.

I checked the clock and when I saw there was only two minutes before the final bell of the day I nodded and yanked my phone out of my bag. She'd actually sent me four texts but I'd been listening to the lecture — unlike Marnie who never listened.

*Bored.* That was the first text.

*Soooo bored.* Second text.

*This class is stupid.* Third text.

*Oh god I can't stand this uber bored what u doing after school?* Fourth and final text.

The bell rang and desks scuffed the floor, making loud grating noises, and students bolted from the room. Marnie stood and waited for me to gather my things. First I had to write down the homework assignment from the blackboard. Yes, I was the keener, the one who wanted the 4.0 GPA. I had big plans for my future that included college and medical school.

"I've got a free night," she said, dancing with her shoulders as she said it. "No volleyball. You wanna go to the mall and a movie? The new one with Ryan Gosling is supposed to be amazing. It's based on a true story. I think a few of us are going."

My phone's alarm beeped and I glanced at it. "I can't," I said. "I have a meeting for the Best Buddies club and tons of homework."

She furrowed her eyebrows. "You're joining that?"

"Yeah." I shrugged. "It's a new program and the first in any Erieville high school. But it is in schools all across North America. It'll look good on my resume."

"You and your resume." She rolled her eyes. "You decide on your university yet?"

"I want to get out of the cold. I'm thinking University of California. They have a great science program."

"I'll visit you," she laughed. "Text me later, okay? After the movie, I might need help with my math."

"Sure," I said. My alarm beeped again. "I've got to get going. I don't want to be late for something like this."

I shoved my books in my bag, stuffed my phone in the top pocket of my jean jacket, and sprinted down the hall to the room where the meeting was taking place. Upon entering, I noticed that there were only around ten people so far. I was five minutes early. I found a seat near the front.

Justin, the Best Buddies chapter president, acknowledged me with a simple hand gesture. I'd met him at a booth he'd set up to raise awareness for the program at the beginning of the school year. I initially went over because I thought he was sort of cute in a blond, brooding kind of way. The entire time I talked to him he never smiled, as if he had some deep entrenched secret that made his entire life dark. For some weird reason, I was drawn to his black mood and wanted to find out what it was that was bothering him so much. I wanted to get him to laugh out loud or at least smile.

Today, his blond curly hair hung to the nape of his neck and his blue eyes looked like pools of water that needed to be de-iced. One day I'd see those eyes crinkle in the corner. One day.

I smiled at him. He nodded and looked away. I had told Marnie about him and she said he'd transferred from another high school just this year and she didn't know his story yet.

The room started to fill up and I looked at everyone as they walked in and I also scouted out the ones who were already seated. Of course Erika was here. She made me smile. She was born with Down syndrome and was a school star because of her sunny disposition. I'd love to be hooked up with her. We could do tons of fun things together. I recognized a few other kids and then there were those who definitely didn't run in my circles, like the girl with the tattoos and severe piercings and Curtis the jock. I'd heard he'd been put on some community service for a fight.

I saw a tall skinny boy with short brown hair enter the room and almost run to a desk as he muttered to himself. He sat down and started rubbing the desk with an anti-bacterial wipe; he could be a classic case of autism/Asperger's or OCD. They had said the Buddies in the program could include kids born with Down syndrome or Williams syndrome or autism or even Fetal Alcohol syndrome. Once I got my Best Buddy assignment I would have to do some research so I could figure out the best way to work with whoever I was paired with. I tapped my pencil on the desk. It would be all about research.

Justin started the meeting and I turned my attention to the front of the room, pulling out a notebook and pen. He explained the program and how it was supposed to work and it sounded easy, just a few hours every other week, going for coffee or a movie or wherever the Best Buddy wanted to go. When he talked about all the special events, I made a note to sign up for the first one because my first semester was academically easier than my second semester.

I loved that Mrs. Beddington was part of the program as she was one of my favourite teachers. Every year, I would make an appointment with her, before I set my academic schedule, just to make sure I was taking all the necessary subjects to get me into a top university for my undergrad science degree. When she said we could see her as early as tomorrow morning to find out who our Buddy was I pulled out my phone and quickly added a meeting with her to my schedule.

Justin ran a short and sweet meeting, and as soon as it ended I bee-lined it to the front of the room.

"I'd like to sign up for that first dance," I said to Justin. "Sounds like fun." I used my shoulders to talk, just like Marnie did, hoping I looked cuter than I was.

"Here's the sheet," he said *without* a smile.

"Per-fect," I said. I signed the sheet noticing that I was the first name and the only name. Maybe just the two of us would work on this. Now, that would suit me just fine.

When I got home from school, I walked in the side door of my house to the smell of Chinese food takeout.

"Mom!" I plopped my bag down and walked into the kitchen. The takeout food was still in paper bags and my mom sat at the table with notes and heavy textbooks spread all over the table. "What are you doing?" I asked.

"Working. A case has me stumped and I need to go through some transcripts." She pressed her fingers against her temples then rubbed them in circles.

"I went to that Best Buddies meeting today," I said, getting plates from the cupboard.

"Oh, okay," she said, without looking at me. My mom was a judge and obsessed with her job. I was her one and only child and she'd had me by artificial insemination. Yup, dear old dad was basically just a sperm donor. Nothing else. I'd never met him, of course. Oh, but I did know that he was Japanese because my mother told me that much and well, it was kind of obvious. She always told me she went for the smartest and healthiest donor — looks and ethnicity weren't a big deal. And I guess I secretly liked the way my eyes and hair made me different from her, made me my own person. At the age of thirty-five my mom had wanted a kid so she'd just had one. That was my mom to a tee, always getting what she wanted.

"The Best Buddies program looks as if it could be interesting," I said.

"Good," she said, still distracted. "It will be great for your resume. Just don't get too involved, otherwise it will take away from your studies." She stared at her notes, scratching her head, and shifting her gaze back and forth across her pages. Suddenly, her eyes lit up and she tapped the table. "There it is."

"Good for you," I said under my breath. Now maybe she would take some time to actually talk to me. Snooping in the brown bags, I saw cashew chicken, beef and broccoli, sweet and sour chicken balls, and chicken fried rice. I put all the lukewarm plastic containers on the table and pushed a plate over to my mom, just in front of her books. She was still gloating over her Eureka-moment as I prepared my plate of Chinese food, noticing that she had forgotten my favourite dish, lemon chicken, even though I had texted to tell her. It was the only one I ever asked for.

I started eating without her.

A few minutes later, she pushed her notes to the side and started to stack her plate with food. "How did your math test go today?" She shovelled in a forkful of rice. Takeout is a staple in our house and so is talking about my school work.

"Good," I said. "I think I aced it."

"That's my girl. Get your 4.0 and you'll get into Princeton."

My jaw tightened as I ground my teeth together. She was always on me about Princeton. "I've been doing some research," I said, knowing I had to choose my words carefully. "I think I would rather go to the University of California in either Los Angeles or Berkeley. Or Queens. They're my top three."

"Absolutely not. I don't want you going to any of those schools. U of C schools are party schools and Queens is for engineers. You need Princeton or Yale or Harvard. That will help you get into Oxford. That's what I've been saving our money for these past few years, after all."

My throat dried and suddenly I wasn't hungry anymore. We always got into an argument when we talked about where I was going after high school. My mother had been a Rhode's Scholar. I knew she'd been putting money aside for me to attend a top school — I went to public high school because she said it was more important to use her money to send me to the best university. Okay. Whatever. I understood that and didn't care if I went to private school or not. But now I was practically an adult and wanted to go the university of my choice, not hers.

I ate a few more bites, picked up my plate, and put the remains in the garbage. "I'm going to my room," I said.

"Study hard. And don't forget who'll be paying for all this education."

Although I was up early my mother was gone before me. The lonely mornings were when I wished I had a brother or sister I could talk to instead of just hearing the refrigerator running, the furnace humming, and the cat snoring. Sometimes being an only child with a single, obsessed mother sucked. I grabbed a granola bar and an apple and headed out to my car. The cool autumn air brushed against my skin and I put my mother to the back of my mind. I was leaving for college in a year anyway.

As soon as I got to the school, I went to Mrs. Beddington's office door. I knocked and said, "Hello?"

"Come on in." Her voice sounded pleasant from behind the door.

I pushed it open. "Morning, Mrs. Beddington."

She smiled at me, making me feel important. "Anna, you're an early bird today. What can I do for you?"

"I was wondering if you had my Best Buddy assignment."

"Have a seat," she said, rolling her chair over to her filing cabinet. "You're the first one to check in." She turned and winked at me. "And why should that surprise me?" She opened the drawer, scanned through her files, and pulled out a green folder, before rolling back to her spot behind her desk.

She opened the file and read it before she looked over at me. "You are going to be paired with a boy named Harrison Henry. He has high-functioning autism which, when I started this job, used to be called Asperger's. I paired you with him because he likes science, and that is one of your interests too."

"I guess that's a good ice breaker for us," I replied.

"He's a lovely boy with good verbal skills, in grade ten, but young for his age. But he comes from a supportive family, which, believe me, is so important for these teens."

"That's good," I said. It made me wonder how my mother would have reacted to a child with autism. I pulled a fresh notebook out of my backpack and clicked on my pen. After labelling it *Best Buddy*, I opened to the first clean page and wrote down the word *austim*, then beside it put *high functioning*. From all my reading, that was going to be important.

"I'm not sure if you know much about high-functioning autism," continued Mrs. Beddington, "but many get fixated on a topic and Harrison's topic is the human body, especially bones."

I scratched down the words *human bone fixation*.

"He knows all the bones in the body and when he's nervous or agitated, he tends to recite them. He also knows muscles and systems and talks a lot about medical diseases, viruses, bacterial infections — oh, and he has a major germ phobia."

As I scribbled down everything she was saying, I thought about the boy cleaning the desk with the sanitary wipe. I would lay bets he was my Buddy.

"He likes *Grey's Anatomy* and movies too. He has an older brother in the school and his name is Joel. I think Harrison's parents want him in the program so he can learn socialization skills instead of relying on Joel for everything."

I wrote down *Harrison's brother is Joel Henry.* "I think I know Joel," I said, looking up. *Of course I knew Joel.* Every girl in the school knew Joel Henry. He was the hottest guy for sure and captain of the hockey team. But...*I'd* never talked to him, and *he'd* never talked to me. He was definitely out of my league and I was sure he didn't even know my name.

"He's popular," said Mrs. Beddington.

"That's stating the obvious," I said with a little laugh.

She smiled at me. "Stereotypes do still exist in high school," she paused. "I'm going to give you Harrison's home number. You call him first and set up a time when the two of you can do something together. My suggestion is to start off simple."

I pulled out my phone and logged his number into my contact list.

Mrs. Beddington looked down at her notes. "It does say here that you shouldn't drive with him in the car. His parents will drive him or make arrangements to have him driven."

"Okay," I said. I wrote that down. *No driving Harrison.*

She closed the file folder and looked at me. "Because of his social skills, he might not want to go to the dance but I think that's the kind of thing his parents really want to get him to try."

"For sure," I said. "I'll work on that one with him." I would make that my first task.

Mrs. Beddington smiled at me. "If you have any problems

or issues, come and see me. Maybe talk to his mother as well. She is very open and honest about Harrison. It's not easy having a child with autism. She's been through a lot."

"Would you have her name?"

"Trudy and Bill. The number I gave you is a home number. Harrison is not allowed a cell phone as of yet. He plays too many games and doesn't get his work done." A knock on Mrs. Beddington's door made me stand.

"Thanks," I said.

"Have fun," she replied. "I know you'll enjoy Harrison."

I left as another student was filing in. I ducked out and headed down the hall, and when I passed the rotunda area I saw Marnie, Emma, and Kara, all holding paper coffee cups. Someone had done a coffee run. I was jealous.

"How was the movie?" I asked them.

"You gotta see it," said Kara, her eyes lighting up. "One of the best I've seen in a long time. Now I want to read the book. I just wish I didn't have so much homework." She moaned and made a face.

"I hear you," I said. "Pleasure reading is not on my agenda anymore." I paused. "Maybe I'll go to that movie this weekend," I said. "With my Best Buddy. I'm paired with Joel Henry's brother."

Marnie raised her eyebrows up and down. "Lucky you. Maybe he could escort you guys. He's so hot." She narrowed her eyes. "I've seen him with his brother. He's always talking to himself."

"Harrison has high-functioning autism." My phone beeped and I pulled it out, reading a text from Justin.

*can u meet at lunch to talk about the dance?*

I fired off a quick *yes* just as the first bell rang. "See you guys," I said to Kara and Emma.

Marnie playfully punched me as we walked toward our first classroom. "If you need someone to join you with your Best Buddy and *his brother*, you know you can count me in."

"I don't think that's how it works." I laughed.

Classes went fine and I did ace my math test. My mother would be happy. At lunch I scanned the cafeteria for Justin. When I spotted him sitting by himself at a table near the back, I made my way over to him.

"Thanks for coming," he said, unwrapping some type of meat sandwich.

I sat down. "Who else is on our committee?" I ripped the wrapper on my granola bar and took a bite.

"It's just us today," he said. "Another Best Buddy couple signed up, Gianni and Erika, but neither of them can make it. I wanted to get things rolling though. Halloween will be here before we know it."

"Erika is sweet," I said. "She'll be great to work with." I paused for just a second before I said, "I got my Best Buddy's name this morning from Mrs. Beddington."

He glanced at me and he had the most amazing blue eyes but they were closed off and unreadable. "Harrison Henry," he stated. "I saw Mrs. Beddington's match-ups."

I nodded. "I'm going to do some research and try to learn more about his type of autism."

"Their brains work differently," he stated gruffly. "You can research but Harrison might not exhibit all the symptoms. Being gentle and kind goes a long way."

"Does your Best Buddy have autism too?"

He glanced away and shook his head. "I'm not going to have a Buddy."

"Why not?" I asked. "I would think that is why you offered to head up the program. So you could work hands on with someone."

Again, he shook his head. "The pairing worked better without me having one."

"We could share," I said. "If that's allowed. I think that would be the best part of the program, getting to know someone with this kind disability and learning how to help them. Maybe you could join us sometimes."

He put up his hands. "I'm fine," he snapped.

"Okay." I paused for a second. "Maybe we should discuss the dance." I pulled out some paper to take notes on.

"Good idea. It should be after school, for two or two and a half hours max." he said.

"Sure," I said. "Will they dress up?"

"Some will. Others might find a costume to be too stimulating."

"I get that. I'm not a huge costume person."

"I'm thinking we should hold it on a Tuesday or Thursday after school. And we could do decorations but keep them minimal. And maybe we can come up with some fun, cheap ideas for snacks and even put up a few activity tables with games and stuff. It could give some of them a break from the stimulation."

"Sure," I said, getting excited. "I can do the food. My friend's mother once made a punch with eyeballs in it. She put blueberries in lychees and they bopped at the top of the punch. Or you can make faces made of crackers and pepperoni. Or cauliflower is great and can easily look like guts."

"Wow. You're getting into this," he said. "Now, just so you know, some might have aversions to certain foods and colours." He tapped his pencil. "I will talk to Mrs. Beddington about that."

Aversions to colours? I wondered about Harrison. Mrs. Beddington didn't mention anything about colours to me. I wondered if I could ask Harrison or if that would be the wrong way to approach him. "When you say aversion to colours, what do you mean?"

"They might get freaked out with too much of one colour." He paused absently for a moment. After a few seconds he shrugged and looked back in my direction. "We need to be careful with the sugar snacks," he said. "Halloween candy is probably not a good idea."

"Sure," I said. "Let me come up with some ideas. And I can do the grocery shopping for this because I have a car." I paused. "When I talk to Harrison, would it be appropriate to ask him if he doesn't like a colour? Or should I try to find something out like that from his parents?"

"You could ask him," said Justin. "He might want to tell you why he doesn't like it. When are you going to call him?"

I shrugged. "Sometime tonight."

"Just an FYI that he could be waiting for your call, and the longer you put it off, the more anxious he might become."

"Thanks for the advice," I said, eyeing him. "You sure know a lot."

He closed his book. "I think that's about it for now. I'll relay this info to Gianni and Erika." A little inkling of a faraway smile crept across his face. "Enjoy every moment," he said. "They're all individuals. And special."

# CHAPTER THREE
## HARRISON

The phone rang but I continued watching *Grey's Anatomy*. It rang again. The shrill sound irritated me. The show went to commercial so I put my hands over my ears but I still heard the phone ring but at least it didn't sound as loud with my ears covered. I didn't want to answer it. I couldn't answer it when I was watching *Grey's Anatomy*.

I was in the family room, sitting on our brown sofa, on the end, in the same spot I always sit at from 3:30 to 4:30 when *Grey's Anatomy* is on. One of the portable phones was beside me because it is always beside me and it was vibrating in its cradle.

"Harrison, answer the phone," said my mother from the kitchen.

"No," I replied. "It is only 3:45."

"Oh for goodness sake." I heard her mutter, but she picked up the cordless phone. "Hello."

My arms were by my side and my hands started to flap. *Flap. Flap.* Up and down. Faster. Faster. Was it my Best Buddy on the phone?

The doctors labelled me a flapper. Not everyone with my

type of autism flapped and I knew that some rocked; I'd seen them in the doctor's office or in the groups my parents used to make me go to. I didn't like going to the groups. Others banged their heads. One girl picked at her head all the time, which grossed me out. And then some kids didn't do any physical gestures. But I flapped. *Flap. Flap.* I knew I should sit on my hands but that took so much concentration and I would have to focus hard to keep them underneath me and I wanted to watch *Grey's Anatomy* after the commercial and only concentrate on it.

My mother walked in front of me with the phone in her hand. *Flap. Flap.* She held it out to me. "It's for you."

I shook my head.

She walked away. "Do you think you could call back after 4:30?" said my mom to whoever was on the phone. "He's watching a show."

The commercial ended and *Grey's Anatomy* came back on and it was the *Time Warp* episode, which was my favourite from season six and I'd seen it 112 times because it had an AIDS theme. My hands stopped flapping when the show returned to the screen. I like *Grey's Anatomy* because of the medical information although sometimes they do stupid things in the show like kiss. Once I wrote the network a letter and told them to stop kissing because kissing can cause things like mononucleosis and herpes and hepatitis B and they should know that because the show is set in a medical facility and the writers should be aware that germs spread, especially in hospitals.

At 4:30 the show ended and my mother came into the family room and stood in front of me again. "Harrison," she said, "that call was from your Best Buddy at school. She sounds really nice."

"She?" My hands started to flap. What if *she* was the girl with the high heels?

"Yes, a she. I take it you didn't go see Mrs. Beddington to find out who your Buddy was."

"What if *she's* the girl with the high heels?"

"You have to get over the high heel thing, Harrison. Girls wear them. They like them. They make their legs look nice."

"There are 26 bones in the foot. That means of the 206 bones in the body, 52 come from the feet. That means that 25 percent of all bones in the body are in the feet. Wearing high heels puts pressure on the three cuneiform bones: the medial, intermediate, and lateral. I can show you exactly what bones are in the feet." In my room, I had lots of photos of the bones of the body on my bulletin board. And I had a plastic skeleton that I'd received for Christmas.

"Harr-i-son." Sometimes when my mother said my name she said it in three syllables. When she sounded it out like this she often dropped her chin, exhaled, and closed her eyes. I didn't know why she got to close her eyes and not look at me when everyone was always trying to get me to look people in the eyes. I waited until she opened them because she always did and that's when I looked down at my lap. "Harrison, look at me. It's important for you to make eye contact."

I glanced up. "Perhaps you should phone the girl back," she said. "I wrote down her number."

That was long enough. I stared at my hands again. "I thought she was calling me back? I heard you say that she should call me back after 4:30."

"Look at me again, okay?" She spoke in a soft voice so I did. "It might be nice if you called her," she said.

"But you told her to call me, so why would I call her?"

Mom raised her hands. "Okay. Wait for her to call then."

I sat back down on the sofa, right by the phone and waited. I started to flap. *Flap. Flap.* The phone didn't ring and didn't ring and I kept staring at it. "Sit on your hands," I whispered. "Sit on your hands."

Mom came back in the family room. "You don't have to stare at the phone like that. Maybe you should go do something else. Do you have homework? I can help you with it."

The phone rang; the shrill sound hurt my ears again so I put my hands over my ears. My mom stood in front of me *again.* "Harrison," she said. "Answer the phone."

I shook my head.

She picked up the phone and said, "Hello." She paused before she said, "Yes, he is. Hold the line for a second." She handed the phone to me. "It's for you."

My hands started to really flap. Up and down.

"Take a deep breath," she said.

I did what she said and breathed exactly how the psychologist had told me to breathe. In through the nose, count to three and out through the mouth, count to three.

"That's good, Harrison," said my mother in her soft voice. "Breathe again."

I did. My flapping subsided. She handed the phone to me. "Talk to her."

I took the phone. "Hello, my name is Harrison Henry."

The voice on the other end said, "Hi, Harrison. My name is Anna and I'm your Best Buddy."

"Did you wear high heels to the meeting?"

"Um," she said. "No, I don't think so." She said 'no' like it had more than one 'o'. Like *nooooo*. I'm not sure why she did that because there is only one 'o' in no.

"I probably had flat shoes on," she said.

"There are twenty-six bones in each foot: talus, navicular, cuboid, and three cuneiforms bones, the medial, intermediate, and lateral. And there are five metatarsals and fourteen phalanges."

My mother shook her head, and waved her arms and mouthed the words, "No. Don't talk about the bones."

"Thank you for telling me that," said Anna on the other end. I wondered what she looked like. "Perhaps we could go for coffee and you could tell me more," she said.

"I don't like coffee," I said. "What colour were your shoes?"

"Um, I think they were pink Tom's?"

"Why would you wear shoes with someone else's name on them?"

This time my mother did this slashing gesture to her throat and whenever she did that she wanted me to talk about something else. We'd had a big discussion on this gesture because at first I wondered why she would do something like that to her own throat. Now that I understood what it meant, I wondered why she didn't want me to talk about shoes.

"Suggest that you go for an ice cream with her," she whispered. "You like ice cream."

"Would you like to go for ice cream?" I asked.

"Sure, that sounds good," Anna said. "Would you like to meet at school tomorrow? Just to say hi."

"I can meet you at 8:23 at the front door. I always arrive at school at 8:22, and I would be able to talk to you for two minutes before I have to go to class. I have to be at the door to my first class at exactly 8:28 or I might not get the desk at the front, which is where I always sit."

"Okay," said Anna. "That works. I will meet you there. Bye, Harrison."

"Bye, Anna."

I pressed the end button and put the phone back into its holster. I felt good about what had just happened. Maybe I was going to have another friend at school. My only friend in high school was Alan and we'd been friends since grade two when he moved in down the street. Joel didn't count as a friend because he was my brother. Alan, my only other friend, was short because of a gene mutation in his body. I wondered if Anna was short. Or if she wore glasses.

"That was great, Harrison," said my mother. "You did well talking to her."

"I wonder if she's short."

My mother squished her eyebrows together. She always does this when I say something she doesn't understand. It makes her eyes look really strange and lines appear in the middle of her forehead.

"Why would you say that?" she asked.

"I only have one friend, Alan, and he's short and now I might have two friends so maybe they will both be short."

"Sit down for a second, okay?" she said. "I want to have a little chat with you."

I did what she asked and sat on the sofa but not in the same spot where I sat when I watched *Grey's Anatomy*.

At first she picked the lint off the black stretchy pants she was wearing and I wondered why she wanted me to sit beside her if she was going to just clean up her pants and try to make them lint free which, as far as I could see, would take a long time. I didn't wear anything with lint or clothes with tags.

"Harrison," said my mother. "You are fifteen now and you have what is called *hormones* in your body."

"I know," I said. "Hormones are chemical substances that act like messenger molecules in the body."

"That is the medical definition but when hormones appear in a teenager they can make you act in a different way, especially around girls. All of a sudden, you may feel as if you want to touch a girl. This can be inappropriate."

"I don't like people touching me so why would I want to touch a girl?" My hands started to flap. I didn't like this conversation.

"You are entering manhood, Harrison, and because of your hormones you might suddenly find that you are attracted to girls."

I didn't like hoods because they always felt as if they were pulling my head backwards so I wasn't sure what she was talking about. Not all men wore hoods. When I became a man I didn't have to wear a hood. My dad didn't have any sweatshirts in his closet with hoods. Joel wore hoods sometimes, but mostly when he exercised and sometimes when he went out at night and it was cold out.

"There are appropriate ways to touch girls and inappropriate ways," she said.

"I don't like hoods," I said. "I'm not going to be a man with a hood."

My mother pressed her fingers to her temples. When she did this it meant she didn't want to talk anymore because she had to think about something. I just sat there and waited for her to finish thinking.

"Okay, let's forget about the manhood thing," she said. "Let's get back to the hormones. Hormones might make strange things happen to your body. For instance, if you think a girl is pretty, you might want to touch the girl. And that could be inappropriate if you touch her on her privates or on her breasts. Do you understand?"

I didn't answer that question because I was still thinking about the word manhood and I thought I had it figured out. "Yes, I understand what you were talking about in regards to manhood," I said. "You were talking about my penis having a hood. If a man is not circumcised then he has foreskin over his penis and it doesn't look like it has a hood." I was feeling pretty good about myself for figuring this one out.

My mom shook her head and said, "I'll let your father deal with this." She stood up. "Dinner is almost ready."

As she was walking to the kitchen, I heard a thud. When I looked over to see what had caused the noise, my mom was on the floor. I rushed over to her just like a First Responder would do.

"Darn," she said, rubbing her ankle. "I wasn't watching where I was going and tripped over the hassock."

I squatted down to look at her ankle. It didn't look swollen or red. I'd seen broken ankles on *First Responders* and they usually swelled up. "Can you move it?" I asked. "The bones of the ankle are the tibia, fibula, and talus."

She rolled her ankle around and around and didn't scream in pain.

"I don't think you broke a bone," I said. "But I'll get some ice from the freezer. That should help it feel better. Ice reduces swelling." I wanted to help my mother just like a doctor would. After high school, I wanted to go to medical school and become a neurosurgeon and although some people laughed and said I would never be able to do that my parents and Mrs. Beddington said I should try to be what I wanted to be. I stood and she also stood, but I noticed she was a bit wobbly. "I think you should sit on the sofa for a minute," I said.

"I'm sure it's fine," she said. She started walking back and forth, shaking it out.

"Ice would really help, Mom. I'll get it for you. It will prevent swelling."

She looked at me and smiled. "Thanks, Harrison. You're such a good boy."

My dad walked into the mud room from the garage at 6:13 and I was helping Mom set the table. She had iced her ankle and now it seemed fine. She said it didn't hurt, which made me happy.

Every day, I set the table. I put the placemats down first, then the plates, then the silverware, forks first followed by knifes and spoons, and I make sure everything is lined up. I get paid twenty-one dollars a week to set the table seven days of the week. If you average that out, I make three dollars every time I set the table. At first my parents wanted to give me twenty dollars but when you divide seven into twenty there is no answer, so I didn't want to get paid twenty dollars. I wanted to be paid either twenty-one dollars or twenty-eight dollars because seven also goes into twenty-eight four times. When my dad suggested that

I should only be paid fourteen dollars, I said that wasn't enough because seven into fourteen is only two dollars and I thought setting the table was worth more than two dollars a time. I also negotiated that if we ate out I still got paid.

"Hi, Harrison," said Dad. "How was your day?"

"Mom fell and might have hurt her ankle," I said. "I gave her some ice to prevent swelling."

"It's fine, Harrison," said my mother. "Don't worry about me." She looked at my father. "Seriously, I'm fine. Harrison was an excellent caretaker. Now, tell Dad about your Best Buddy, Harrison."

"My Best Buddy's name is Anna and we are going for ice cream." I put the last plate on the table.

"Good. That's really good." My dad looked at my mom and when he did he held up his thumb. I knew this meant he was happy about something because Joel had taught me that. I was to put my thumb up if I liked something.

My dad gave my mom a kiss on the cheek. Kissing the cheek is different than kissing on the mouth because there is no saliva exchanged. My parents used to kiss on the mouth but not anymore because once I had a meltdown when I actually saw the saliva with my eyes and heard sucking sounds, and since then they don't kiss like that anymore. They must have realized it could give them germs and perhaps bacterial infections or viruses, unlike Joel who didn't know that yet. When I was little I had a lot of meltdowns and my mom hated it when the meltdowns happened in Walmart but I couldn't control where we were or when it happened, and that's the truth. I work hard on trying not to have as many meltdowns because in high school it isn't a good thing. Yes, it is *inappropriate*.

"Go get changed," said my mom to my dad. "Joel just texted and he should be home any minute now."

I wanted to correct her and tell her that it couldn't be *any* minute because time was specific so it had to be *a* minute. For instance, Joel might be home at seven minutes after six or eight minutes after six. But he wouldn't be home at *any* minute because he couldn't be home at seven minutes after five because that minute had already happened. But if I said anything I was quite sure she would squish her eyebrows together and perhaps have to put her finger to the middle of her forehead.

Joel arrived home at eight minutes past six and I liked that because eight is a good number. Dad came back downstairs dressed in sweat pants and a t-shirt but no hood. Then I remembered that the hood my mother was talking about had to do with the penis. My brother Joel had a hood on his penis but I wasn't sure about my dad. I'd never seen his penis because I didn't like being in a bathroom when someone else was in it and I didn't like anyone being in the bathroom when I was in it. Being at school all day is hard and I hold my urine until I get home (unless I'm desperate — then I go outside and urinate by a tree) because once I went in the restroom at my elementary school and got my head pushed into the urinal and had a huge meltdown. After that incident they let me use a special restroom, but at the high school I was told I had to use the public one because it was something I had to learn to deal with.

I helped my mother carry the food to the table because I was still thinking about her ankle. I know that sometimes fractures in bones show up later on an x-ray. I'd seen that on television. I wasn't sure that would be the case with my mother but I thought it would be a good idea for her not to walk too much. I didn't look at the food, of course, because sauce covered the chicken and I don't like sauces on food.

We sat down to dinner and I ate chicken and rice and green beans but the others ate the chicken dish with tomato sauce and cheese on top. I don't like sauce and I don't like my food touching so my mom made me chicken, rice, and beans.

"Harrison found out who his Best Buddy is," said Mom to Joel.

"Oh, yeah. Who?" Joel shoved food in his mouth. Joel eats a lot and he eats anything and he loves sauces and sometimes he eats with his mouth open and I don't like that because I can see the food all mixed together. I looked down at my plate so I wouldn't have to see inside his mouth.

"Her name is Anna," said my mom. "Do you know her? I think she's a senior as well. She sounded nice on the phone."

"There's a super smart girl in my grade named Anna."

"Smart. That's good," said my dad.

"Yeah," said Joel. "Like a genius in science."

"What if she wears high heels?" I asked.

"High heels are sex-y," said Joel. "If it's the same girl I'm thinking about, she's good looking in a sexy-smart way. Nice body too."

"Joel," said my mother. "We don't need to hear all your specifics."

"There are twenty-six bones in each foot," I said. "High heels can hurt the bones of the feet. Sexy is the word sex with a 'y' on the end of it." Words were swirling in my brain. I didn't like that I didn't know what Anna looked like.

"Let's change the topic," said my mother. "How was hockey practice today, Joel?"

"AIDS can be transmitted through semen and vaginal secretion and can be transmitted through unprotected sex," I said because I had to get the words out of my brain. "I learned that on *Grey's Anatomy*, on the *Time Warp* episode, which I watched today. It's my favourite episode."

"Harrison, I said no medical stuff at dinner," said my mother. "Let's talk about the Best Buddy program and some of the things they do."

Joel laughed. Loudly. "Yeah, let's talk about Harrison and Anna. Maybe she can be your girlfriend, Harrison."

"Joel, stop it," said my dad, shaking his head.

My hands started to flap. I didn't want a girlfriend because we would have to hold hands and kiss and I didn't want to share germs. "Kissing can cause things like mononucleosis and herpes and hepatitis B." I said my words quickly so my mom couldn't tell me to be quiet. I know I wasn't supposed to talk about medical stuff at the dinner table but I had to. I had to get the words out of my brain or they would just continue to bounce.

"New topic." I knew my mother was looking at me and she almost sang her words.

I was staring down at my food but I couldn't really see it because in my mind I could see Joel and the girl in the hallway, kissing, and saliva was on their mouths. "Joel almost kissed a girl in the hallway and he might get mononucleosis or Herpes." I spoke without looking up.

"I did not," said Joel. I could tell by his tone of voice that he was not happy that I'd said something about him and the girl in the hall.

"Who was the girl, Joel?" my mother asked him.

"You know he can't always read a situation properly," said Joel. Then he said, "Maybe, just *maybe*, Harrison will kiss a girl one day and figure out it's actually not that bad. In fact it's fun!"

My hands flapped. I didn't like this conversation. And then, *boom*, there was too much going on in my head. That's how it happened. Everything piled up. I'd never met Anna. I didn't want to hold her hand. Or kiss her. What if she was a girl who wore high heels? Fast. Faster. *Flap. Flap. Flap.* I could feel my brain filling up, spinning. Words bounced everywhere. Words like *kiss* and *germs* and *kiss* and *germs*. What if she *kissed* me?

"Joel! Stop it, now." My mother raised her voice at him. I don't like it when she raises her voice. Yelling voices hurt my head.

"Harrison," said my father. "Slow down. And breathe. Or sit on your hands."

My hands flapped and I couldn't stop them. I knew I should sit on them but the words were swirling in my brain so fast that now I couldn't get my hands underneath me. I couldn't speak either because the words were spinning too fast for me to get to them and say them out loud. Around and around. They were caught in a spin cycle and wouldn't stop. My hands were flapping and flapping.

"Look what you've done now," said my mother to Joel. "Why do you have to antagonize him?"

Joel stood and when he did he pushed the table. My plate slid across the table and landed on my lap.

"I'm always the bad guy!" Now Joel was raising his voice too.

I looked down and all my food was mixed together: chicken was with beans and beans were with rice and rice was with chicken. I heard myself screaming as I thrashed my arms and legs to get the food off my body because it was all mixed up. Dishes crashed to the floor and sauce landed on my pants. Sauce! I hate sauce. I didn't want it on me. The sauce landed on the chicken and the beans so I flung my arm to get it off.

"You know how he reacts," said my mother.

"I always get blamed for everything in this house." Joel yelled.

Sauce landed on my bare arm. My skin burned. "It's on my arm!" I screamed. "Sauce is on my arm!"

I flung my arms and it made me fall to the floor and the loud thud bashed against my head. Everything swirled in my brain. And I heard myself screaming.

And screaming.

And screaming.

I had to get the food off of me.

# CHAPTER FOUR
## ANNA

At 8:15 in the morning, sipping a takeout coffee from Starbucks, I leaned against the concrete wall in the front lobby of the school. Last night, I'd done a ton of research on Harrison's type of autism, and so far, it seemed as if he could be a textbook case. I made sure I had set my alarm to get up and arrive at the school early. Something like being late might cause him to be upset. From our phone conversation the night before, I deduced that time was something he obsessed about, that and bones of the body. I figured that when we went for ice cream, I would listen to him talk about bones to break the ice and I could tell him that he was prepping me for university and medical school.

I yanked out my phone and checked my text messages. One from Marnie.

*hey doll, can u meet at lunch i'm dying in math.*

I smiled to myself. Marnie and I couldn't be more opposite. I guess that's why we were friends.

*sure*

We texted a little more about trivial stuff then she sent one that told me to tell her the second I met Joel. I smiled to myself. Of course, she would want to be introduced.

Even though I had half of my coffee left, when I saw it was 8:21, I walked over to the trash can and threw the cup out. I remembered Harrison saying he didn't like coffee so I didn't want to start off on the wrong foot with that either. At exactly 8:22, Harrison walked up the sidewalk to the front entrance. I glanced around for his brother but didn't see him anywhere.

I waved when he walked through the front doors. "Harrison," I said.

He glanced quickly at me before he lowered his head and walked over to me.

"Hi," I said. "It's good that we can meet."

"Yes," he said without making any eye contact. I noticed his hands moving at his side, almost as if they were a bird's wings and he was trying to fly. Mrs. Beddington had told me he was labelled a "flapper."

"I'm looking forward to going for ice cream with you," I said.

"I think it is important for you to know that I used to have Asperger's," he said in this factual, robotic tone, "but this has been changed to high-functioning autism. When I was first diagnosed all the doctors told me I had Asperger's. I'm not sure why they changed it but I feel this is important for you to know so you don't get confused. When would you like to go for ice cream?" he asked. "My mother told me that is something I should ask and that I shouldn't talk about the bones of the body."

"When we go for ice cream you can tell me about the bones," I said. "I don't mind."

"I watch *Grey's Anatomy* every day at 3:30. It would be impossible for me to go at that time."

"I like that show too," I said.

"Yesterday's episode was *Time Warp* and it is my favourite episode from season six. I know you can't get AIDS from sipping out of a straw because saliva doesn't transmit the virus."

"I'm glad you told me that," I said. Oh dear, this was awkward. He didn't know how to talk to me, but I also didn't know how to talk to him, and that needed to change. "Um, we could go for ice cream after you watch *Grey's Anatomy* or later in the evening if you eat supper at a specific time." I said.

"My dad always comes home just after six and I'm usually finished dinner by 6:30. Sometimes he comes home at 6:03 and sometimes at 6:05. He is unpredictable and I don't like that. But I set the table every day and make twenty-one dollars a week so I would have enough money to buy you an ice cream. My mother said I need to buy your ice cream as this is the appropriate thing to do."

"That's so sweet of you," I said. "But I can also treat you too sometimes. When would you like to meet?"

He didn't say anything and I could see his hand flapping increasing in intensity. "My mother will have to drive me," he said.

"Okay, well, you check with her. We can also meet on a weekend. Maybe on Saturday."

"I would like to meet on Saturday." His hand flapping slowed a little.

"Great," I said. "That works for me. How about 2:00 pm? Then we will have had lunch."

He nodded. "I have to go now," he said. "It is 8:24 and I have to be standing at the door of my class by 8:28 to get a seat at the front."

Near the end of first period, I remembered that I had told Justin I would meet him at lunch to go over plans for the Halloween dance. After glancing at the clock and seeing that there were a few minutes left before the bell, I texted Marnie and she wrote back telling me that I *had* to meet her. So I texted Justin and asked if he could meet after school because something had come up for me at lunch. Within seconds, I had a text back telling me after school was fine.

When I walked in the library at lunch, Marnie had her books spread out in front of her and looked frazzled. Her curly red hair was thrown back into a high ponytail and tendrils fell all over her flushed face.

"Wow," I said. "The library."

"Shut up. I have to do well on this exam today. And I don't get it." She sat back in her chair and moaned.

I sat beside her and perused her notes. "First off, you don't have the right equation."

"What?" She sat forward again and stared at her notes.

We worked for the entire lunch period and by the end, Marnie had a little more of a grasp on what she was doing, although she probably wouldn't ace the exam. Just saying.

As we gathered our bags, she said, "So how's the Best Buddy thing going?"

"Good. I'm meeting with him on Saturday for ice cream."

"The brother?" She raised her eyebrows up and down as she shoved, and I mean *shoved*, her books in her bag.

"No." I rolled my eyes at her.

"Oh, by the way — I found out a little about that Justin guy. Rumour has it he got into some brawl at his old school and got kicked out and had to transfer to our school. We're the only school that would take him."

"Really? A brawl? What for?" I used my hands to quote the word 'brawl.' In a way it didn't come as that much of a shock: the guy *did* have this brooding look about him at all times.

Marnie shrugged. "I didn't get *that* much info. Be grateful for what I got." She hip-checked me as we walked out. "It would do you good to hook up with a bad boy."

Justin had his head bent over his books and was scribbling on a piece of paper when I walked into the cafeteria for our after-school meeting. He had suggested we meet in the cafeteria; if I had been thinking at all, I should have suggested going for coffee to maybe lighten him up a bit, get him away from the school. Once again, his solemn face gave me no indication that he was happy to see me.

"Hey," I said, sitting down across from him. "What are you working on?"

"Chemistry."

I nodded. "Who is your teacher?"

"Rowlands."

"I've got Smyth. I've heard Rowlands is tough but a good teacher. He's supposed to explain it well."

He threw his pencil down and groaned. "Yeah, and I still don't get it."

"I might be able to help you," I said.

For the next fifteen minutes we worked on his chemistry homework and when he had the final answer he looked at me and tried to smile. I knew he had it in him. "Thanks," he said.

"No problem. Anytime." And I meant it.

He closed his books and pushed them to the side, so I pulled out a file folder with recipes I had printed off for cool Halloween party treats. "Look at all the fun stuff I found for food. Eyeball punch. Carrot fingers sticking out of dip. Cheese and cracker faces. We could set up an awesome fun food table." I slid my notes over to him.

He flipped through my pages. Last night, when I was thinking of ideas, I had remembered as a kid going to a Halloween party at a friend's house, and her mother had made a ton of treats like these ones. I had been so excited because my mother never did stuff like that. She made me quit going out for Halloween when I was eleven, saying I was too big. I had to hand out candy at our house.

"What do you think?" I asked.

"I like some of the stuff, but we will also need simple stuff like a basket of crackers, cut-up cheese, a veggie tray. Food mixed together can be an issue."

"Sure," I said. Sometimes I felt as if I knew nothing about kids with developmental handicaps. I thought I'd done my research, but then Justin would say something that my research hadn't told me. "That's cool. We could keep the tables separate. Have a Halloween type table and a plain table." I wondered about Harrison. How he felt about his food mixing up.

"I met up with Harrison this morning," I said. "It was brief but we are meeting for ice cream on Saturday. He doesn't like coffee."

"Me neither," said Justin.

"Would you like to join us?" I thought I would try again because I felt bad that he didn't have a Best Buddy.

"No, that's okay."

"Do you have any more tips then that might help me deal with him? I was a bit awkward this morning with him. I don't want to be."

"If you give him the freedom to talk, he probably will. And don't touch him. Sometimes touching can set them off. It's a sensory thing. Some have issues with noises, some with smells, and others have tactile issues."

"Did you do a paper or project on this?" I asked.

He shook his head. Then he looked at me and the ice in his eyes had melted and all I saw was sadness. Before I could ask anything else, or find out why his mood had suddenly changed, he glanced at his watch, and closed his books. "I've gotta go," he said.

On Saturday, I wore jeans and flat shoes but not the pink ones because I didn't want to confuse Harrison. I drove to the ice cream place, parked my car, and looked at the time. Five minutes early. Should I go in and get a seat? Or wait outside? Why was I so nervous? I remembered what Justin had said about letting him do the talking. I was good with that.

Maybe it would be best if I went in and waited for Harrison. I got out of my car and that's when I saw a silver car drive into the parking lot with Harrison in the front seat and his mother in the driver's seat. After they talked for a few seconds, he opened the door and stepped out. I wondered if his mother was going to talk to me but she didn't get out. I wasn't sure if I should introduce myself or not. Feeling awkward, I made no attempt to move forward. Harrison shut the car door and walked over to me.

"Hi, Harrison," I said.

"Hello, Anna. My mother is picking me up in exactly thirty minutes. She feels that will be long enough for our first meeting. I told her I didn't want her to meet you because I want to do this by myself and I'm feeling quite capable today. She told me not to be inappropriate but I told her I thought she was being inappropriate to bring that up when I hadn't even been inappropriate yet. She also told me to breathe if I started to spin. I have to breathe in through the nose, count to three, and breathe out through the mouth and count to three. You might have to do the same thing if you start getting mad and want to yell at me. I don't like it when people yell at me. Joel yelled last night at the dinner table. Sometimes he has to breathe in through his nose and out through his mouth and he doesn't always count to three because he is impatient. I brought a ten dollar bill with me and I would like to buy your ice cream. I don't like mine in a cone."

*Whew.* The guy could talk. Like, *really* talk. I wondered if it was my turn now.

"I don't either," I said, before he could start up again.

We went into the ice cream store and there was a line-up of only three so I figured it wouldn't take long. To my dismay, Harrison put his head down, walked right to the counter and said, "I would like two scoops of vanilla in a bowl, please. I have money to pay for two people."

An older gentleman who was the next in line said, "Young man, you have to wait in line like everybody else. Kids these days." He harrumphed in disgust.

I didn't know if I should tell him to get in line with me. The fact was: Harrison did look like every other teen his age. From the outside no one could see that his brain was wired a different way.

A lady holding the hand of a little boy leaned toward her son and said, "We always wait in line, don't we?" She straightened up and I heard her mutter, "Why can't parents teach their children manners?"

I noticed Harrison's hands starting to flap by his side. I had no idea what to do. I remembered the breathing, but how would I go up to him and tell him to breathe? Should I?

Harrison looked at the lady and I felt my heart start racing. Oh no. Was he going to start something here in the ice cream store? Before I got to him to tell him to breathe? *Oh, God, please no.* My own breath became shallow and panicky. I didn't have a clue what to do if a fight broke out. It's not like he was a small kid; he was a young man with muscles.

"I'm sorry," he said to the man.

"I'm sorry," he said to the woman.

"I'm sorry," he said to the boy.

Then he walked to the back of the line.

I heard the man up front mutter, "Smart ass."

I knew I should tell Harrison to breathe but when I looked at him he was doing it on his own and rather loudly too.

"Do you want to sit outside when we get our ice cream?" I asked him, using a quiet tone. I thought perhaps outside would be the best place for us to sit because there was less stimulus, not so many people.

"Yes," he said. "The temperature is twenty-one degrees today, which is higher than the average temperature for this time of year."

Perhaps I could keep him on the temperature topic. "What is the average temperature for this time of year?"

He rambled some facts off for me and it kept us in the line and allowed the people ahead to order their cones.

All the ice cream flavours were written in chalk on a board hanging on the wall. I scanned it to see what kind they had and saw there were so many to choose from — some really good ones too, like Dutch Apple Pie and Key Lime Pie. I thought about what Justin had told me about aversions to colours and foods mixing. Harrison had said he wanted vanilla.

"Is vanilla your favourite?" I asked when it was almost our turn.

"Yes," he said. "My mother likes chocolate and my father likes Tiger Tail. I don't like the black in the Tiger Tail but my father tells me not to look at his ice cream. So I don't. And Joel likes maple walnut. I don't like nuts in mine because the mixture of foods doesn't work."

Harrison ordered his vanilla and, because he had said his mother liked chocolate, I ordered a plain dark chocolate, no nuts, no marshmallow, no cherries, just plain chocolate. Harrison paid. When he got his change, he stood at the counter, even though there was a line-up behind us, and started counting the change the girl had given him. I could feel the energy of the people behind me, and they were impatient.

"Next," said the girl, even though Harrison hadn't moved yet.

He finished counting, oblivious to the muttering going on behind him, and we headed outside, finding a table in the sun. A warm breeze whisked through the air and the sky was clear, the colour of sapphires.

"Mrs. Beddington told me you were interested in the bones of the body," I said sitting down. I wanted to get the conversation rolling, plus I didn't know what else to talk about.

Instead of answering me, he sanitized his hands using a little bottle he pulled out of his jacket pocket. Then he dug into his ice cream. With his head lowered toward his bowl, he ate every spoonful without speaking then he got up and put the bowl and plastic spoon in the trash. At this point, I was only halfway through my ice cream.

As soon as he sat back down, he pulled out the hand sanitizer again, and rubbed his hands over and over and over. He was going to peel away a layer of skin if he didn't stop soon.

He must have cleaned his hands for at least a full minute before he started reciting the bones of the feet. It was as if a switch had gone on in his brain. I listened in amazement. His brain had stored a lot of information. Once the bones of the feet were done, he moved to the bones of the lower body. I ate my ice cream and listened to him list all 206 bones in the body in a matter of minutes.

"That's great you know all those bones," I said, scooping up the last of my ice cream.

"I have a plastic skeleton at home. It is in my room."

"Like the ones at school?" I asked.

"Yes. I got it for Christmas two years ago."

"Is science your favourite subject?" I asked.

"Yes. But I don't think I'm going to like it when we do

the physics unit because I don't like physics as I find it hard to understand."

"What about English?" I asked.

"I have a tutor for English and I don't like him. He smokes cigarettes and cigarettes are harmful for the body."

I was about to say I agreed with him but he launched into a litany of why cigarettes were bad and what they did to the lungs. Again, I listened.

When he was finished, I wanted to take a breath for him or tell him to just take a moment to catch his breath but he continued talking. "I want to be a surgeon one day," he said. "But I would have to finish high school, go to university and get a BSc, then apply to medical school by writing my MCAT. I would have to go to medical school for four years, including a residency in the hospital, get licensed, and specialize in neurosurgery."

"We have something in common," I said, almost butting in. "I want to be a pediatrician."

"My mom says if I want to do this, I will have to get over my touching issues but neurosurgeons wear gloves."

"Yes, they do," I replied. I wondered about his touching issues. I had read that many autistic kids had sensory issues.

"My mom almost hurt her ankle the other day and I helped her so I think I can do it."

"That's good," I said. "Is she okay?"

"Yes. She didn't break any bones or hurt the ligaments surrounding the bones. I gave her some ice to prevent any swelling." He stood and said, "I have to go now. My mother is here."

I stood too. "Bye, Harrison," I said. "That was fun." And

that was the truth. It had been interesting, informative, and also fun in a different-fun kind of way. I watched Harrison, with his slouched shoulders, walk to the silver car. Before he got into the vehicle, however, he looked up and down the street, three times, one way then the other, all deliberate movements. I wasn't sure what he was hoping to see but after the third round he did get in his mother's car, do up his seat belt, and talk for a few seconds to her.

I bent forward and waved to her and she waved back. I wanted to tell her that we'd had fun, that Harrison had been great, and he really was sweet. I wanted her to like me and know that I was going to be a good Best Buddy for Harrison. I watched as the car pulled away. I think I'd been successful with him. I'd let him talk, like Justin had told me to do.

As I unlocked my car and got in, I wondered about how to get him to go to the Halloween dance. This might be a whole lot harder to do than I thought. But it was my job in all of this. I had to get him to go. That was all there was to it.

# CHAPTER FIVE
## HARRISON

The traffic was moderate as I scanned the road. Both sides seemed to be moving slowly and were not congested. Sometimes on a Saturday, traffic could get heavy, with everyone out shopping for groceries and clothes. I didn't like shopping for clothes so my mother brought things home from the mall or from Walmart and I tried the clothes on in my bedroom with the door shut and if I liked how the fabric felt on my body, she didn't have to take them back.

My mother liked me to sit in the front seat of the car with her because she said I needed to learn how to ride in a car with just one other person and that meant sitting in the front. That was *appropriate*.

"So?" my mother asked, after I had my seat belt done up. She knew not to talk to me until I had it snapped in place. "How did it go? Was she nice? Did you pay for her ice cream like I told you to?"

"That's three questions," I said. "I can't answer all three questions at once."

"I'm sorry," said my mother. "Let's do one at a time then. How did it go?"

"I ordered vanilla."

"Was she nice?"

"I don't know."

"Did you pay for the ice cream like I told you to?"

"Yes."

My mom pulled away from the curb and I didn't like how fast she was going. I glanced at the speedometer.

"You're going three kilometres over the speed limit."

"What did you talk about?"

"Bones," I said.

"Harrison, I told you to try and talk about something else."

"Watch out for that girl on the red bicycle!" We had to pass a girl riding a red bicycle. I didn't like red bicycles. I had one when I was little and my parents tried to teach me how to ride it and I kept falling and one time after I fell I jumped on it and broke all the spokes and my parents got mad at me. Dad yelled and threw the bicycle in the trash, and Mom said he shouldn't have done that because a bike repair store might be able to fix it, and Dad said what was the use, I would probably never learn to ride it anyway. And I never did.

I didn't want to pass the girl on the red bicycle. What if she fell and jumped on her spokes and my mom yelled at her and she threw her bike in the trash? The girl was on my side too and our car had to go right by her. We might get too close. We might hit the girl on the red bicycle. I clenched the dashboard. "Watch out for the girl on the red bicycle! I don't like red bicycles."

"That's enough," said my mom. "I'm not going to hit the girl."

"You're going to hit the girl on the red bicycle and she's going to fall and jump on her spokes and you're going to get mad because you're going three kilometres over the speed limit. I don't want to be in another crash with you."

Mom veered the car over to the side of the road and, after she braked and put the car into park, she opened the glove compartment and pulled out my Nintendo DS. "Go in the back," she said. Her voice was quiet and soft and not like Joel's when I was in his car and he threw me the video player. She handed the DS to me. "Don't look at the road."

I did as she asked and got into the back seat. The rest of the ride I played my video game.

The television was blaring from the family room and I heard it as soon as I walked in the house. I lined up my shoes on the shoe rack. Joel was in the family room, lying on the sofa with his arms over his head, watching a television show or a movie, wearing sweat pants and a sweat shirt with no hood. He wasn't allowed to go out today with his friends and could only go to his hockey practice because my parents had said he'd come in too late last night. They were wrong about what time he'd come in though and he hadn't come home late at night, he'd come home early in the morning, at 3:02 am.

My parents weren't happy with Joel because he was experimenting with alcohol. They'd been mad at him and yelled and the yelling woke me up and I don't like yelling. For once Joel was happy that I don't like yelling because I came out of my room and told everyone to shut up. He gave me the thumbs up and that meant that he was happy with me. His breath had really smelled.

"Hey," he said. "You want to watch television with me?"

"I don't know," I said. "I don't like scary shows or ones where cars chase each other."

"We can watch what you want," he said. "Only, not *Grey's Anatomy*. I can't hack another rerun."

He sat up and started flicking through stations. "Tell me when you see something you like."

The shows flicked one after the other and I didn't see anything I liked and Joel kept flicking. "See anything?" he asked.

I shook my head.

"Okay, let's watch this. It's a teeny bopper show. It might help you learn about life at high school. Some kids your age watch shows like this." He stopped flicking and put the remote down. He also stretched his legs out on the coffee table and crossed his ankles.

I sat in my spot but it didn't feel right because I wasn't watching *Grey's Anatomy*.

"How was ice cream with that girl?" Joel asked.

"Her name is Anna and I ordered vanilla."

"What did you talk about?"

"Bones. Mom said I shouldn't but Anna said it would be okay."

Joel shrugged. "She's a whiz in science so she probably didn't mind. With girls you have to figure out what they like."

"She likes chocolate ice cream because that is what she ordered. I ordered vanilla because that is what I like."

"Good on yah for noticing what kind of ice cream she ordered. Oh, look," he said, pointing to the television. "The kids on the show are going to a dance. I heard your Best Buddies program is going to have a dance for Halloween. You should go."

The boy danced with the girl on the television show, and they were moving slowly and going in circles under a light that flashed and flashed. They were close and the girl leaned her head on the boy's shoulder and he moved his hand up and down her back like he was playing a recorder. In school I'd had to play a recorder once but mine kept squeaking and squeaking and the sound made me anxious so the teacher let me stop playing but everyone else had to keep playing. I went out in the hall with a special teacher. That happened a lot. I've had a lot of special teachers. A fast song played on the television now and the boy and girl pulled apart and danced fast, moving their arms and legs in funny ways.

"Dances can be fun," said Joel. "When the song is slow you have to ask a girl to dance. But when it's fast you can dance with anyone."

I kept watching the television. "What if I ask someone to dance and she's wearing perfume? Or high heels?"

"You can see the high heels on the girl so if she's wearing them don't ask her. Personally, I think high heels are sexy and it's time you got over that one. As for the perfume, sometimes it's strong so you can smell it before you ask. If it's too strong don't ask her. But don't go sniffing the air in front of a girl. That would be a no-no."

On the television, the girl grabbed the boy by the shoulder and pushed her face towards his and kissed him.

My hands started flapping. "What if I ask a girl to dance and she tries to kiss me?" I said.

"Trust me," said Joel, laughing. "One day some girl is going to kiss you and you're going to like it."

"I don't want to have her saliva in my mouth." The two teens on television kept kissing and I could hear the sucking noises. I closed my eyes and put my hands to my ears.

I felt Joel's hands on mine, pulling them away from my ears. "Hey, Bud, relax, okay? It's normal to want to kiss a girl," said Joel.

My hands, loose now, started flapping again. "I could hear the saliva being exchanged," I said. "That is not a good thing. It causes—"

"Breathe, Bud, breathe," Joel interrupted. "It's not a big deal. Let's change the station."

Joel flicked on a station that had a commercial about laundry soap and my hands slowed down.

"Don't worry about kissing a girl just yet," said Joel. "Just dance with one first."

"What are you boys watching?" Mom asked from the kitchen. Mom's ankle was fine today, she said, and there was no swelling so I was happy she could walk around without being wobbly.

"Don't you worry, Mama Bear," said Joel. "Me and my Bud are doing some male bonding."

When the show came back on, Joel's phone started to buzz and buzz, one text message after another, and that's when he left the family room to go to his room. Today, I had a friend, just like Joel. I went out for ice cream with Anna, my friend.

I picked up the phone and called a number I knew by heart.

"Hi, Alan," I said. He is my other friend and he is short because he has Achondroplasia, a bone growth disorder. We both have disorders that start with the letter A, so that was why in grade two I wanted him as my friend. No one really knows what mine is caused from but Alan's is caused by a gene mutation in the *FGFR3* gene. In grade two when I met Alan, I looked up what was wrong with him because it had something to do with his bones. The *FGFR3* gene makes a protein called fibroblast growth factor receptor 3 that is involved in converting cartilage to bone. I told him this at school and at first he got angry with me but then we became friends. I never cared that he was short but in elementary school the other kids said mean things to him and called him midget and dwarf because Achondroplasia is also called Dwarfism. The kids at school nicknamed us Dork and Pork. Obviously, I was the dork. Once I tried to tell them that I had *Asperger's* (that's before they had changed Asperger's and put it in with autism) and he had Achondroplasia and we weren't Pork and Dork but that made them laugh even harder.

"Hi, Harrison," said Alan.

"I have a new Lego Star Wars Mind Storm Developer kit. Would you like to come over?"

"Really? When did you get that?

"I bought it with my birthday money."

"Wow. Cool. Let me ask my mother."

I waited for Alan to come back to the phone. Alan lives two doors down so no one has to drive him when he comes over to my house and no one has to drive me when I go over to his house. But I don't go to his house often because there are always dishes in the sink and clothes on the floor and milk rings on the kitchen counter. I don't like it there and once I had a meltdown so my mom said that I should always have Alan at our house because that would be better for everyone.

"I can come," said Alan. "For a few hours. Mom said I have to be home by four o'clock."

I went to the kitchen to get a drink of water. Books were spread on the table and my mother was busy making stencils of letters. My mother is a kindergarten teacher but she just went back to work a few years ago. When I was little she stayed home with me and when I was in grade school she worked part time but sometimes she had to leave work to come to my school because I was having a meltdown.

"Alan is coming over," I said.

"Oh," she said. "You're having a busy day." She looked at me over the rim of her reading glasses. "Are you sure this is a good thing?"

"It's okay. I can handle it today. I would help you with your stencils but Alan is coming over." I often help my mother make things for her classroom because I like that she works with kids. My grade one teacher, Miss Campbell, had been nice to me, and Alan too, and didn't let the other kids in the class tease us, and I know my mother is a good teacher who helps all her students like that.

"That's okay," she said, cutting the construction paper. "I would rather you be with a friend."

The doorbell rang two minutes and forty-seven seconds later and I answered it. "Hi, Alan," I said.

Alan walked in and took off his sneaker shoes but he didn't line them up. He never does, just like Joel. We went up to my room and I pulled out the Mind Storm box from under my bed. I hadn't started building it yet because it needed to be done on a Saturday when I had time. When we were in elementary school Alan and I built huge bridges out of Lego but now we were into building Lego robots, which are a lot harder and require concentration. Alan sat down on the floor and reached out to touch the box but I pulled it away from him.

"Sorry, I always forget." He laughed and took the bottle of hand sanitizer from the small table beside my bed. I wanted a dispenser installed in my room but my mother said that would be ridiculous. Every time she went for groceries she had to buy me a new bottle so I thought having a dispenser would have been a good idea and not a ridiculous idea. Alan used the hand sanitizer to wash his hands.

Once I knew his hands were clean I opened the box.

"I went for ice cream with a girl today," I said, handing him the directions. His job was to read them aloud. Mine was to listen and figure out which part we needed.

"A girl?" Alan stared at me. "Did you like, go on a real date with a real girl?"

"No," I said. "It was not a date. It was a Best Buddy meeting at the ice cream store. I had vanilla and she had chocolate. She is my Best Buddy and her name is Anna."

"I thought you hated joining things. You won't join the Lego Mind Storms Club with me."

Alan had asked me to join the Lego Mind Storm Club at school but I had said no.

"My mom said Best Buddies would be good for me and she made me go," I said. "Most meetings are only with Anna so it is a one-to-one meeting. I like that. Sometimes I have to go to a meeting with more than just Anna but not that often. With the Mind Storm Club, every time they meet there are too many people."

"But that's what makes the Club so awesome," said Alan.

"Everyone shares ideas. The robots we're building are wicked."
He picked up the directions and glanced at the paper. I thought
he was going to read aloud our first directions but instead he
asked, "Is Anna pretty?"

Why did he want to know if she was pretty? And what
was *pretty*? Was Amy pretty? The girl Joel shared saliva with on
the sofa? Or Beth? The girl in the school hallway.

"She has black hair and brown eyes because she's part
Asian," I said. "Her hair is straight and she wears flat shoes."

"There's one girl in my Mind Storm Club who I think is
really pretty." He had this weird look in his eyes and I didn't
think he was thinking about building a difficult Lego robot.

"Maybe you can go for ice cream with her one day." I
tapped the paper. "Read the first direction."

"Not if my mom keeps bugging me about being
homeschooled. She loses her brain when kids are mean to me
and she always says she's gonna pull me from school."

I didn't want Alan to talk. I wanted him to read the
directions.

"A kid in grade eleven pushed me the other day," continued
Alan. "We got sent to the office. They called my mom and she
freaked."

"I hate going to the office," I said. "Read the directions."

Alan picked up the paper but he didn't do like I asked.
Instead he said, "I told her I wanted to stay in school because
of the Lego Mind Storm Club. We might go in a competition in
the spring. Sometimes I wish my mom didn't want to baby me
so much. I keep telling her I'm in high school now and I can
take care of myself." Alan put the paper down and looked at me.
"Are you going to go out with Anna again?"

"I have to if she is my Best Buddy, Alan. My mother wants me to go to a dance with her. I might not go."

"A dance? Cool."

"Read the directions," I said.

"If you go to the dance with a girl," said Alan, "when the slow song comes on, you have to dance close. I saw that on television."

I tapped the page.

"And she'll probably want you to kiss her. I saw that on television too."

"I'm not going to kiss her," I stated. "I don't want to exchange saliva." Just the thought of kissing a girl made my skin itchy. I picked up the hand sanitizer and squirted it on my hands. "I don't think I'll go to the dance."

"Dude, go," said Alan. "I'd go if I were you."

"Kissing causes bacterial infections or mononucleosis, which comes from the Epstein-Barr virus." I tapped the paper for the third time. "Read the first direction."

Finally, Alan read aloud and I listened carefully before I pulled out the first piece we needed for our robot.

# CHAPTER SIX
## ANNA

The brochure for the Science Centre sat on the top of the junk mail pile that was ready for the recycling bin. I picked it up. Why didn't I think of this before? I could take Harrison there. We could spend more than thirty minutes and we wouldn't have to talk the entire time. I knew for a fact there was a human body section and they had interactive games to name the bones and a giant plastic skeleton.

"I wish they'd stop sending us junk mail," said my mother, pouring herself a coffee. She drank coffee morning, noon, and night. Right now it was eight in the evening. I don't know how she could sleep later on; I would be buzzed all night. My mother kept a wacky schedule. Sometimes I could hear her in the middle of the night, downstairs doing work.

I waved the brochure. "Every once in a while there is a diamond in the rough."

"That is a bad cliché and I'm not sure you used it correctly," she said. "Please, don't use it in your English essay. Good way to lose marks. By the way, how'd you do on that last essay?"

"95%." I answered.

She took the brochure from my hand. "The Science

Centre?" She laughed. "That's for little kids."

"It's not for me," I said. "I can take Harrison there."

"Who is Harrison?" She stirred sugar into her coffee. "A boyfriend? You don't have time for a boyfriend."

"No," I snapped at her. "He's not a boyfriend. I told you about him. He's my Best Buddy."

"Right." She leaned against the counter and sipped her coffee. "He's the boy in that program that will look good on your resume."

For some reason, I didn't like the way she said that, as if he were *just a number*, to use another bad cliché. "He's also a human being," I retorted.

"I know," she said. She blew out this big rush of air. "I'm sorry I said it that way. It's just that I see kids like him every day in court. They can't cope so they do drugs, get violent, and end up in prison or a mental institution."

"He has good parents, a support system. He copes."

"I've seen many who come from good families derail." She shrugged as if she knew *everything*. "They still fall through the cracks. It's sad."

"You can't generalize like that, Mom. *Some* don't fall through the cracks. Some go on and become brain surgeons. I've done a ton of research."

She held up her hands. "Okay. You're right. I guess in my line of work, I just see the ones who don't exactly become the brain surgeons of the world."

"You've been at your job way too long." I said, staring at her, wide eyed. "That's one of the reasons behind the program. It's set up to raise awareness so that all kids have the potential to do something with their lives. Everyone needs a break, you know."

"Did you know that elephants will shun a blind elephant?"

"What is that supposed to mean?"

"Many animal species don't accept disabilities."

"Mom, we are *humans* — not *animals*." Was she for real? Just because she was a judge didn't mean she had the right to, well, *judge*. And to me, right now, that is what she was doing.

"But even though we have the capacity to accept," she continued, "many humans are still like elephants, shunning anyone who isn't normal." She used quotation marks when she said the word *normal*.

"So let's try and change that," I said.

"From what I've seen, our trying doesn't seem to be working," she said with a sigh.

"Well, some of us have to keep trying then."

"This visit today means that I have been to the Science Centre 888 times," said Harrison as we put our tickets in the machine to get scanned and then walked through the turnstiles to get to the exhibits. "My mother is picking me up in three hours. I caught the bus to get here."

"That's great. Do you catch the bus often?"

"Only when my parents or brother can't drive me. My mother teaches kindergarten and she had parent-teacher interviews tonight and my brother has hockey and my father is out of town on business."

Were we making progress? This was shaping up to be an actual conversation. "Does your dad travel a lot?"

"Yes. Sometimes he's even gone on the weekends. They

have a new exhibit today on the digestive system."

"Did you want to go directly to the human body section?" I asked.

"Yes."

He picked up his pace and walked ahead of me so that I almost had to run to keep up to him. I deduced that his mind was fixated on getting to the new digestive system exhibit. Had he really been to the Science Centre 888 times? I had been here maybe 10 times and that included elementary school trips. To my surprise, the first display he approached was the plastic replica of the human skeleton and Harrison stared at it, mesmerized, as if it were a golden statue. He picked up the head set and listened. I watched him become still, calm, and it was as if he listened and focused with his entire body. Guaranteed, right now, I was not on his radar. Oh well.

Time ticked by and Harrison stayed in concentration mode. We didn't communicate at all; no 'hey, listen to this' or 'Anna, come see this.' He might as well have been at the Science Centre by himself. He listened to the speaker as if he was in a lecture and he was going to write an exam tomorrow on the information, and the exam was the most important thing in his life. Yes, I might have that level of fixation when I write my MCAT exam one day, but not when I'd heard the same voice before — 888 times. He knew this stuff off by heart with the exception of the one new exhibit.

Repetition and ritual.

He moved to a plastic structure that showed all the muscles.

I went to the new digestive exhibit. As I listened to the man talk about digesting food, it reminded me that I hadn't eaten supper. Just thinking of food going through the digestive system made my stomach grumble. There was no food in my house. My mother didn't grocery shop much, so plastic takeout containers and cardboard boxes littered the kitchen.

Sometimes I wondered why she had me. It was as if I had been some experiment and after I was born she figured it wasn't an experiment worth repeating. Nor did she want to observe the growth of the experiment. My only hope to keep her interested in me was to make it to medical school.

Harrison moved from one exhibit to the next. Another hour passed and I wanted food. Plus, to be honest, I was bored. My stomach kept rumbling so I watched Harrison closely, just waiting for him to remove the head set so I could approach him and get him to leave. His focus never wavered and I wondered how I was going to get his attention. Did his mother snap her fingers in front of him? Or perhaps she could touch him. Maybe he didn't have sensory issues. I remembered Justin telling me that touching him *might* set him off but then again, it might not if he wasn't sensory sensitive. I sure as heck wasn't going to touch him and find out that he did have sensory issues, not when we were in a public place. I watched him carefully, and finally the moment happened and he took off his head set. I moved in for my kill.

"Harrison," I said. "Are you hungry?"

"Yes," he said.

"Good," I said. "Because I'm starving. My stomach is growling."

"Stomachs don't growl," he said. "Animals growl. Stomachs make noises. The digestive system starts at the mouth and ends at the anus, and is like a tube that connects organs and passages. Peristalsis pushes food downward in waves of muscle contractions. The food gets churned and mixes with liquid and digestive juices and is called chyme, a semifluid mass. Sometimes pockets of air and gas mix and they create the noises. This doesn't only happen when you're hungry. Sometimes it happens when you have a stomach full of food." He glanced at his watch. "My mother will be here in 58 minutes."

"Um, we have time to go next door," I said. "There's a cute little café."

"I like the cafeteria here at the Science Centre," he said. "They have hot dogs. I can eat bread and meat together without worrying about how it is going to go through my digestive system."

The thought of eating a chewy hot dog or a gross hamburger with wilted French fries at the cafeteria in the Science Centre was more than I could stomach.

"I bet you could find something to eat at the restaurant too," I almost begged. "It might be good to get some fresh air."

"I would like to go outside," he said. "I'm hot."

The restaurant was only a block away so when we got outside I walked in that direction, hoping that he might give in. Was I pushing? I looked at him as he walked, and he had his head down, per usual, but he was walking, and also talking to himself. He was saying 'walk,' so maybe he wanted to walk to the new restaurant. Maybe the talking was helping him cope with a new situation. So far, he seemed to be following.

The street wasn't too busy, just a few people and a couple of cars. We could probably get a table tonight. As we approached the red awning of the restaurant, I slowed down, taking smaller steps to give him time to process something new.

"This is the restaurant," I said, trying to keep my voice cheery. "Let's look at the menu first."

He stepped forward and read a few words then stepped back. His body went stiff and he just stood like a pole in the middle of the sidewalk. "I can't go in there," he said, his voice sounding strangled. "They serve sauces on everything. I can't eat sauces, especially red sauces and white sauces and cheese sauce. I don't like pizza. I don't like spaghetti with sauce but I like spaghetti by itself. White sauce is gross and I've never seen a pink sauce before. I like chicken and rice and vegetables. I don't like sauces. I don't like it when my food touches."

His hands were flapping like crazy and he was getting a stoned look in his eyes. Then he started walking in circles, and it looked as if he had a pattern.

Not good. And it was all my fault for going to my sort of restaurant rather than considering Harrison's comfort zone.

"Have you had enough fresh air?" I asked, hoping to get his focus off my lame idea to try someplace new. "We could go back to the cafeteria."

"Yes. Let's go to the cafeteria now."

The walk back was a lot quicker — as if we were racing against time. Harrison practically left me in the dust.

In front of the food cooler at the Science Centre cafeteria, I pondered a wilted garden salad and a sorry-looking ham and cheese sandwich. I took the salad and ordered French fries. Harrison ordered a hot dog and put nothing on it. Not even Ketchup.

We ate in silence. I let him eat his entire hot dog while I picked at my French fries and salad.

When he was done, I asked, "Did you learn anything new today?"

"I learned about the digestive system."

"I'm glad they had that display today," I said.

"Me too," he replied.

"Would you like a French fry?" I pushed the cardboard tray toward him.

"No, thank you," he replied. "I don't share food." He pulled out his wipes and cleaned the table.

"Oh, well, that's a good thing." I smiled at him and pulled the fries back.

I ate a few more French fries just for something to do and not because they tasted good. Seconds slipped by. Harrison sat across from me, sipping his soda.

"You can't get AIDS from sipping through a straw," he said, putting his empty cup down.

"That's good to know," I answered. I put my napkin over the leftover fries. They were gross and I couldn't eat another one. Harrison started to fidget in his seat and I wondered if he had to go to the restroom or if a tag was bothering him, scratching his skin. Maybe he was too embarrassed to tell me that he had to go. He crossed his legs. Would I embarrass him if I asked him?

"I have to go to the restroom," I said, smiling at him, thinking this was the best way to handle the situation.

He avoided eye contact. "I don't use public restrooms," he said.

"Oh," I said. Too many germs, I gathered.

I excused myself and left him alone at the table. In the restroom, I was quick and made sure I washed my hands for a count of twenty just in case he asked. All in all, I was probably gone for three minutes tops.

But when I returned to the table, Harrison was gone.

# CHAPTER SEVEN
## HARRISON

The outside air whisked my skin, cooling me down right away. I wanted to eat something at the Science Centre cafeteria, not at a restaurant with an awning located on the busy street. Plus I didn't want to be outside because it was much colder than it was when I left the house and I only had one sweater on. Once I was cooled off I thought we should go right back in again. Sometimes I liked being outside, like when it was sunny in the summer and I could play marbles or chess with Alan, or during the first snowfall when I could make snow angels, although, now that I was older I didn't make snow angels anymore.

Cars whizzed by. People walked down the sidewalk. Both ways. Buzzing sounds came from buildings. Electrical noises hissed from the wires above me. There were too many people. Too many cars. Too much noise.

I could smell coffee. And garbage.

I wanted to walk in a circle.

"Let's go for a walk," said Anna.

She had black flat shoes on and not high heels. I lowered my head and looked at my feet. Perhaps I could walk forward instead of in a circle. I could count three steps and three steps. I could do that. Yes, I could. I wanted to stay at the front entrance of the Science Centre, or go inside, and not walk down the street the wrong way. She started to walk and I told my feet to move.

"Walk," I whispered. "Walk. Walk. Walk."

I had never walked this way down the street before, so I didn't know where the bumps on the sidewalk were or if the curbs were being fixed by road crews or if there was a sewer manhole. The bus dropped me off at the bus stop that was located the other way. The first time I caught the bus my mother came with me, the second time my brother came with me and the third time my father came with me. I caught the bus with them each three times, which made a total of nine times. Then I caught it with Alan three times to make twelve times. Each time I walked the same way to get to the Science Centre.

I didn't like walking down the street this way.

"This walk feels good," said Anna. "It will clear our heads."

Clear our heads? If we cleared our heads we wouldn't have brains and that would mean we would be brain dead and in a coma and be hooked up to a ventilator to get oxygen into our bodies, and have a feeding tube in our stomach to eat. Walking wouldn't really clear your head.

Someone went by me and I felt his shoulder against my shoulder. I moved over and almost bumped into Anna. Now I had to move back over the other way. I didn't want to feel someone's shoulder against mine but I didn't know which side of the sidewalk to walk on. Usually, you walked down a street on the right and up a street on the left, but I'd never walked this way so I wasn't sure if we were going up or down. I didn't like anyone touching me, rubbing shoulders with me. Touching burned me and made me feel hot and itchy.

We kept walking.

I kept breathing. In through my nose and out through my mouth.

"Breathe," I whispered. "Breathe."

Anna stopped in front of a building with a red awning and it made me think of the red bicycle. "Let's look at the menu," she said. The menu was on a laminated board on the brick wall outside the restaurant.

My hands started to flap. My brain started filling with words. Menu. Sauce. Red awning. Sauce. Red bicycle. Digestive system. Chyme. Spaghetti and meatballs. Alfredo with garlic sauce. Prawns with a pink, rosé sauce. The words started to spin. My hands flapped faster and faster. I tried to breathe.

"I can't go in there," I said. "They serve sauces on everything. I can't eat sauces, especially red sauces and white sauces and cheese sauce. I don't like pizza. I don't like spaghetti with sauce but I like spaghetti by itself. White sauce is gross and I've never seen a pink sauce before. I like chicken and rice and vegetables. I don't like sauces. I don't like it when my food touches."

I couldn't move my feet to go in the restaurant so I went in a circle. Three steps. Round the corner. Three steps. Round the corner. My hands flapped. I thought, if she goes in I could run back to the Science Centre and wait for my mother to come and pick me up. I'd never caught the bus home and I never went down the sidewalk this way. But I could run back and not stay outside on the street, walking in circles.

"Have you had enough fresh air?" she asked me. And she didn't go into the restaurant.

My hands slowed and didn't flap as much. I breathed in through my nose and out through my mouth and I stopped walking in circles. She turned and walked the other way. We were going back to the Science Centre and hopefully to the cafeteria where I could get a hot dog. I could eat a white hot dog bun with a hot dog wiener. Eating a hot dog wouldn't bother me or make me feel like exploding and having a meltdown. The bun would be soft in my mouth and wouldn't have any nuts or seeds or oats. Buns mix fine with wieners. I wouldn't feel as if I was eating chyme when I was eating a hot dog. I walked as fast as I could so I wouldn't have to go into the restaurant with the red awning.

At the counter in the cafeteria at the Science Centre, I asked for a hot dog with a soft bun. Anna went to the cooler and pulled out a salad and then she went to the grill and ordered French fries. There was a girl with a tattoo and an earring in her nose working the cash register. People with tattoos make my underarms and palms sweat. Sweating happens when I run a lot or walk fast or ride my bike, but it also happens when I see someone with a tattoo or when kids at school push me or take my lunch. Sweat is the body's way of cooling down and it happens when I exercise or get over stimulated. One way makes me wet and the other also makes my throat dry and my heart race too.

I waited by the grill for my hot dog and Anna paid for her food and my hot dog and that was a good thing because I didn't have to give my money to the cashier with the tattoos. My father told me that being a cashier would be a good job for me one day because I'm good with money. It doesn't look that hard and I know there are people who are cashiers and they aren't as good with money as I am.

Once I had my hot dog in its little paper wrapper, Anna and I sat at a table. I cleaned the top of the table off with a wipe I had in my pocket. Biting into my hot dog, I didn't look at Anna's salad because it had lots of different vegetables, including sprouts and I hate sprouts, and red peppers, and it also had cheese and croutons and she put dressing on it. My mom says — well, the doctors too — when I go out to dinner, I'm supposed to ignore what other people are eating and focus on my own food.

I finished my hot dog and Anna was still eating, picking at her food. My mother didn't like it when I picked at my food.

"Did you learn anything new today?" she asked.

The new digestive display had been informative, and although I had known a lot of what was said, I did learn a few new things about peristalsis. But my mother has told me not to talk in detail about the human body.

"I learned about the digestive system," I said. My mother would think that was a good answer.

She slid the cardboard container of French fries over to me and asked if I wanted one. Sharing food, to me, is inappropriate. Using my indoor voice, I told her I didn't share food. Germs could be spread if you shared food or double dipped; I never ate potato chips with dip or corn chips with dip, unless I had my own bowl of dip. Joel loved nachos and cheese with salsa and ate them with his friends and I thought that was gross.

I sipped my soda while she ate a few more French fries. I didn't want to talk to her when she was eating because what if she answered me right away like Joel did and I saw the food in her mouth? That might make me feel sick to my stomach. I kept sipping my drink and sipping. Finally, there was nothing left. The soda made me have to urinate but, of course, there was no way I would use the restroom in a public place. I crossed my legs. Sometimes that helped me and made me feel as if I didn't have to go. Unfortunately, today the urge was extremely strong and wasn't going away. I jiggled my leg.

"I have to go to the restroom," she said.

"I don't use public restrooms," I said.

"Oh," she said, standing up. "I'll be right back."

As soon as she was out of sight, I got up and walked as fast as I could outside. I glanced around, up and down the street, and when I saw a tree around the side of the building, I figured that was as good a place as any. I knew I wasn't supposed to urinate outside on public property, like a building. But a tree would be okay. There was no way I could hold it until my mother came.

I walked quickly to the tree and when I got there I looked around again. A lady was across the street with her dog. Oh no. I shook my leg. I wished she would hurry up. Finally, she moved out of my sightline. I yanked down my zipper and exhaled in relief.

"Harrison!" I heard Anna call my name and it made me flinch.

Urine splashed against the tree. I couldn't stop the flow. It just kept coming out. My heart raced. The palms of my hands started sweating. Urine splashed against the tree and back at me. Some landed on the bottom of my pants. Now I had germs on my clean pants. I didn't want urine on my pants. I didn't want to wear my pants now. I couldn't. It was like wearing underwear with tags.

"Harrison!" she called out again.

I didn't answer her. I couldn't. Not now. She couldn't see me urinating up against a tree!

"There you are," she said in a breathy voice. "Oh, okay." Her voice sounded surprised.

"I guess when you gotta go, you gotta go. I'll wait for you by the front entrance."

Then she was gone. I finished and looked down at my pants. Even in the dark of night, I could see the wet spots. My body started to itch. Taking my pants off in public would be inappropriate. I knew that. Maybe if I rolled my pant legs up the spots wouldn't be touching my skin. I pulled out my hand sanitizer and cleaned my hands first. Then I carefully reached down and, avoiding the spots, and using just my fingertips, rolled up my pant legs until they were just under my knees. Then I cleaned my hands again.

I breathed in and out. Three times. The itching stopped a little. I could do this.

After my third big breath I walked away from the tree and out to the front of the building. Anna was still waiting for me. When she saw me, she didn't ask about why I had my pants rolled up.

"Recent studies have shown that urine is not sterile," I said.

"Thank you for sharing that," she replied.

"I hope you didn't see my penis," I said.

"It's okay, Harrison," she said. "It's pretty dark outside."

"My mother is late."

When my mother pulled up in front of the Science Centre, she opened the front door but I got in the back seat, shut the door, and did up my seat belt.

"Why are your pants rolled up like that?" She handed me my video player.

"You're late. Two minutes and twenty seconds."

"Well, that's hardly late." She pulled away from the curb and I turned on my video player and we didn't talk for the rest of the ride home.

Once in the house, she asked, "Did you have a good time with Anna?"

I put my shoes away and immediately unzipped my pants. "Stomachs don't growl," I said, taking them off. "The noises are made from trapped gases that are in the stomach."

"Why are you taking off your pants in here?" My mother put her shoes in the right cubby. "You should do that in your room."

"I ate a hot dog and she had a salad and French fries and she offered me one but I told her I didn't share food."

"Good for you," she said. "You handled an uncomfortable situation."

"I didn't look at the salad because it had more than one vegetable."

"Harrison, I'm proud of you," said my mother. "You coped." She paused. "You need to answer my question about your pants though. Why you are taking them off in here? And why were they rolled up?"

"They need to be washed," I said.

"Okay. But you have a laundry basket in your room."

"They have urine on them."

"Did you pee your pants?"

"No. I didn't pee my pants. I'm not a baby, Mom."

She put her hand on my shoulder. "May I?" she asked. Sometimes I didn't mind my mother touching me, but if my brain was spinning and I was going to have a meltdown and she asked, I was allowed to say no. One time when I was having a meltdown and she tried to touch me, I hit her by accident. Everyone screamed at me and my dad got upset, and Joel cried, but I couldn't stand how hot her hand felt on my body. It stung me and felt like a bee sting. I'd had a bee sting once and now I don't like bees.

"Yes, you may," I replied.

"I know you're not a baby," she said. "Just explain what happened."

"I drank too much soda and had to urinate so I went outside and found a tree and urine splashed on my pants because Anna called my name and the sound of her voice made me move because I didn't want her to see my penis. That would be inappropriate."

"I think we need to revisit you learning to use a restroom. You can't keep going outside. There's a law and if a policeman sees you, he could fine you."

"I don't want a policeman to fine me and put me in jail."

"Jail is a little extreme. But he can fine you."

"Anna and I had a conversation about the restroom," I said.

"You talked with Anna about restrooms? I would think there would be other things you could talk about."

"She said she had to go and I said I didn't use public restrooms. But then I had to go so badly because I drank an entire soda so I went outside. I couldn't wait until you arrived. You're always late."

My mother pressed her fingers to the lines in the middle of her forehead for a few seconds and I waited until she was finished which took three seconds total so I knew she'd counted to three like the doctor told her to.

"Okay, give me your pants. I'll wash them tomorrow."

I handed her my pants and walked to my room in my underwear.

# CHAPTER EIGHT
## ANNA

Faded jeans showed off Justin's butt to perfection.

"Justin," I called out.

He turned when he heard my voice and I'm positive I saw a hint of a smile on his face. He wore a black t-shirt and his hair had a rumpled sexy look. I moved quickly to catch up to him.

"How's it going?" he asked, pulling the cafeteria door open for me. And who said chivalry was dead? I grinned as I walked in. Noise blasted out the door. Tables were scarce.

"Great," I replied, scanning the big room. "How are things with you?"

"I passed my chemistry test."

I held up my hand and he slapped it and it seemed as if he kept his hand on mine longer than he needed to.

"How's Harrison?" he asked.

At the back of the cafeteria I could see Marnie waving to me. I blew her a kiss and, after a quick glance at Justin, she gave me the thumbs-up and a raised-eyebrow look. A group of students sitting right in front of us crumpled their lunch bags and stood, leaving some room at the end of a long table.

"You want to sit down?" I asked.

"Sure," he said. "I *was* going to study."

I playfully slapped his back. "You need to eat too." We nabbed the table. "Harrison's great, thanks for asking," I pulled leftover pizza from my bag. "We went to the Science Centre last weekend. He loved it. Although, I left him alone for a few minutes to use the restroom and when I came back he was gone. I was so freaked out. I had no idea where he'd disappeared to."

"Where was he?"

"Peeing against a tree. I'm pretty sure he has a phobia about public restrooms. Too many germs perhaps?"

Justin shrugged. "Yeah, could be that. Or he was bullied in one. Lots of bullying goes on in the restroom."

"Good point. Does with girls too," I said. I remembered being in grade nine and not wanting to go in the restroom if the grade twelve girls were in there.

Justin looked down and flicked a few random crumbs off the table.

"He really liked the Science Centre though," I said to change the topic, hoping to get his thoughts back from wherever they had just gone.

He shook his head as if to clear his mind before he looked at me. "If he liked it, take him back. Repeats are great."

"So I gathered. He told me he'd been there 888 times."

A small smile appeared on Justin's face, and I thought I saw dimples. "That sounds familiar," he said.

"In what way?" I asked.

He toyed with his sandwich, a homemade one that looked a lot more interesting than my cold pizza. Nervous that I had pried, I waited for his answer, picking the pepperoni off the pizza and eating it.

"Horses," he said, finally. "Being at the barn. That was her big thing."

"Her?" The one word just popped out of my mouth.

"My sister, Faith." He blew out a stream of air and scratched the back of his neck.

I wondered what school she went to or if she went to school, how old she was — but I knew I had to limit my questions. I just hoped I'd ask the right ones. "Do you guys ride horses together?" I asked.

"We did but it wasn't what she liked best. Her favourite thing was feeding them apples and brushing their hair." He shook his head with this wistful look on his face. "She always wanted me to braid her hair the same way when we got home."

"And did you?" I couldn't help smiling a little as an image of him braiding hair flittered through my mind.

He nodded and this time one side of his mouth lifted a little. "I'm good at it."

I smiled back at him. "That's a skill not many guys have," I said, realizing that this guy was more complicated than I thought. From getting kicked out of a school for being in a brawl to braiding a girl's hair. "Is your sister older or younger?" I took a bite of my pizza.

"Younger," he said. "By three years."

"So she would be a year younger than Harrison," I said. "You must spend a lot of time with her." I paused. "Is she autistic?"

A black-out blind seemed to lower on his face and suddenly I couldn't see in anymore.

"I'd better go study," he said gruffly. And then he was gone.

So much for treading carefully.

After school I met up with Justin and the two others involved in the Best Buddies dance: Gianni and Erika. Gianni was a year younger than me and I didn't know him personally, but I'd seen him in a lunch dance show. He seemed like a nice guy and eager to help. Erika was his Best Buddy and she was as sweet as gumdrops, with her huge smile and crinkly eyes. Unlike Harrison, she loved to hug. When I showed her pictures of some of the food we were planning, she clapped her hands.

The meeting went well and Justin talked to me, but I couldn't get a read on whether he was mad at me for being nosy. In a way it was nice to have some other people at the meeting, to create a buffer between us and also give me time to assess his mood. Gianni was pleasant and full of positive energy and he kept the meeting lively with his animated gestures. He said he would take care of all the decorations, and Justin offered to help me with the shopping for food. That surprised me: a good indication that he wasn't mad at me after all.

Once we picked a date, we talked costumes and activity tables. Erika wanted to be a bunny. At the end of the meeting, after hugs and goodbyes, Gianni and Erika walked out together. I waited for Justin. I had to.

He glanced at his watch. "Darn," he said. "I missed the bus. Now I have to wait another thirty minutes."

"I can give you a ride," I said.

"I don't live around here," he muttered.

"No biggie. I don't have too much homework tonight."

He moaned. "Don't mention homework. I've got tons."

"Let me give you a ride then. You'll get home quicker."

With a sheepish look he said, "Thanks. I appreciate it. I'm not good with this bus thing."

Remembering what Marnie had told me about him getting kicked out of his last school, I decided not to pry about why he wasn't "good with the bus thing." Perhaps his parents took away his car privileges or the police did; there could be numerous reasons why. Or maybe his problem was as simple as his car being in the shop. All I knew was, I wasn't going to ask. Not this afternoon. Not after too many questions at lunch.

As we walked out I said, "I was thinking about asking Harrison if he would like to help with the committee. Do you think that's a good idea? Maybe if he helps with the committee, he will want to come to the dance. He still hasn't agreed to go. It was nice to have Erika here today."

"Erika and Harrison are totally different. But you could ask him. Just don't expect much. He's pretty awkward in social situations."

"Yeah, he is," I said. "But I think I'll try anyway."

"Just remember — what you think is good for him is not always right."

We walked the rest of the hallway without talking. Once outside I looked up at the sun blazing the sky, loving the feeling of it toasting my skin. Autumn. Some days were dreary and wet and others were perfect, like today. The cold weather wasn't quite here yet, but it was coming, and days like today were precious. "Awesome day," I said.

"These were the days Faith liked best at the stables," said Justin. "She loved it when it was crisp." He used his fingers to quote the word 'crisp.' "At first the word confused her and she said that chips were crisp but air couldn't be crisp."

I glanced at him out of the corner of my eye. "Faith is such a pretty name."

"Yeah, it is."

"Look, I'm sorry about today at lunch. I should mind my own business."

"It's okay," he said, shoving his hands in his pockets, hunching his shoulders. "Maybe it's what I need."

"My car is at the end of the lot," I said.

Again, silence hovered between us as we walked to my car, and every little background noise could he heard, including my feet on the pavement and his breathing beside me.

"Here's my baby," I said. I unlocked my crappy Toyota Corolla and we both got in. I started the engine, it sputtered, and I reversed out of the parking spot. "Where to?" I asked.

"Go left," he said.

Usually, I went right to get home but I turned left and he guided me away from the school and toward one of the wealthiest neighbourhoods in the city of Erieville. With the help of Justin's directions, I wound my way through side streets, past huge old brick homes with vines running down them. Old money. Finally Justin said, "It's the house with the blue car in the driveway."

I parked out front.

"Thanks," said Justin. "I really appreciate it."

"No problem."

He opened the car door, then turned to look at me.

"You want to go for coffee or a movie sometime?"

His question stunned me for a second. But it didn't take me long to recover. "I'd love to."

"Maybe on the weekend?"

"That'd be good," I said. "If you need help with your homework tonight give me a call or text."

"Sure," he said. Then he got out of the car, gave me a little wave, and walked toward his front door.

I pulled away from the curb and when I was out of sight, I pounded my steering wheel in absolute joy. "I have a date with Justin," I sang in the car, dancing with my shoulders. Wait until I told Marnie.

All night I hemmed and hawed about asking Harrison if he wanted to help on the committee. If I got him on the committee maybe, just maybe, he would go to the dance. I went online and researched his type of autism again, digging up a few new websites, trying to figure out if it would be an insensitive question.

Why was I being so hesitant? I closed my computer and picked up my phone to make the call. A woman answered and I figured it was his mother. "Is, uh, Harrison there?" I asked, stumbling over my words.

"Is this Anna?" she asked.

I took a quick breath to compose myself. "Yes, it is."

"I'm Harrison's mother, Trudy. Thank you for working with him. We are so appreciative," she said. I heard her exhale and she sounded hesitant, almost nervous too. "I think this program is really good for him."

"It's my pleasure. We had a wonderful time at the Science Centre the other day."

"Oh," she said, "that is *soooo* good to hear."

I detected relief and I wondered what Harrison had said when he got home. Did he not have a good time? Had I done something, said something that made him react when he got home? I was pretty sure I wasn't supposed to let him pee outside. Or pee on his pants.

"Do you think he enjoyed himself?" I asked.

"He loves the Science Centre," she said. "We've been there a lot."

"Yes, 888 times. That's what he told me."

She laughed. "One summer we went almost every day. Finally I had to nix going to the gift store. He loved going in there and wanted something every time. It got expensive."

I laughed at that and it made me relax a little. "That's good to know." I paused for a second before I said, "I have something to ask him but maybe I should ask you first."

"Sure," she said.

"Do you think he'd work on a committee for the dance? I'm organizing the food. He still hasn't decided to go to the dance so I thought if he worked on the committee and was able to make some of the decisions, it might make him want to come. We could get him to help with the activities table. Should I ask him?"

"That last question is an easy one to answer," she said. "Go right ahead and ask him. One thing about Harrison: he's honest. If he doesn't want to do it, he will let you know. But he's not here right now. He's out with his father."

"Maybe I can look for him at school tomorrow," I said.

"Perhaps I could get him to meet you. I will be dropping him off in the morning."

"Okay," I said, "at 8:22."

"Oh yes. Time has to be exact. It's such a relief that things went well for you last time you met."

"So far, so good," I said.

I stood in the front lobby of the school at exactly 8:22 and watched Harrison lope up the sidewalk. For a fifteen-year-old, he sure is tall.

"Hi, Harrison," I said.

"Hello, Anna. My mother said you would be meeting me this morning. I have two minutes to talk because I have to be at the door of my class at exactly 8:28 to get a seat at the front."

"I was wondering if you would like to help me organize the dance. I thought you could help with the activities table. Give me some suggestions." Why was I babbling?

"No," he said. "I don't think that would be a good idea." His hands started flapping at his side. "I don't want to be in a meeting with a lot of people."

My heart sank. The hand flapping alarmed me and without thinking, I reached out and touched his arm to reassure him. When I realized what I'd done, I retracted my hand.

"I'm sorry I asked you," I said, wringing my hands, anticipating a calamitous reaction.

His hands stopped flapping. "You have nothing to be sorry about," he said, to my surprise. "You asked a question. I answered."

Relieved, I burst out laughing. "Harrison, you are so right."

Then he quickly glanced at me, and I grinned when I saw his small smile.

# CHAPTER NINE
# HARRISON

The Lego Jedi robot was built but we had to program it and change a few things to make it better. The basic programming was always too easy. Alan and I had worked a total of four hours and twenty-three minutes on it. Today we'd worked for two hours and twenty-one minutes.

"I'm hungry," said Alan. "Let's take a break."

"Okay," I said, glancing at my digital clock. "We have enough time to eat and finish the robot and try it out. I hope the sword works."

Downstairs in the kitchen, I made Alan some crackers and peanut butter. I made myself crackers and cheese but I put them on a different plate than Alan's so the crackers didn't mix with the cheese. Plus Alan was a messy eater and left crumbs everywhere.

"Did you go for ice cream again with Anna?" Alan munched on a cracker.

"No." I moved my plate closer to me so Alan's crumbs wouldn't land on it.

"That's too bad," he said. "I bet you wanted to, especially if she's pretty."

"We went to the Science Centre, then we had something to eat."

"You ate with her? Amazing. That's a big step for you." He didn't say anything for a few seconds, letting me finish my snack. As soon as I stood to take my plate to the dishwasher, he asked, "Is she like your girlfriend now?"

"She is a girl and she is my friend so, yes, I would say that she is my girlfriend." I rinsed my dish. "She touched my arm today and it didn't bother me."

"That's huge," he said. "For you. What grade is she in?"

"Twelve."

"She's older than you? That means you've got a cougar. I read that when a younger boy goes out with an older woman she's called a cougar."

"She is not a cougar. They are part of the cat family."

He brought his plate over to the sink. "When are you going to *kiss* her?"

"I'm. Not." I shook my head. "I already told you that. Kissing spreads germs."

"Okay. Okay. Are you at least going to that Halloween dance with her?"

"I don't think so. I don't like crowds."

"Dude, you should go. This could be your big chance."

Joel walked into the kitchen with a hairy mask on. It covered his entire head and I wondered if he could breathe. Underneath the mask, he made some noises, like he was trying to growl.

Both my father and mother laughed. I didn't think the

noises were that funny and I didn't think the mask was funny at all. Why would he wear something over his face? I wouldn't want to wear something over my face.

"Where did you get that?" my mother asked Joel.

He took the mask off and his face was red. "At a second-hand store," he said. "Amy is having a house party."

"Perhaps we should talk about this party," said my mother, putting a salad on the table. I didn't like looking at the salad so I didn't. I had broccoli on my plate and chicken and rice.

"I'll behave," said Joel. He plunked down in his chair that was across from me. We sat at the same seats for every meal and I liked that.

"Harrison's the one you gotta watch," said Joel.

"I don't think I'm going to the Best Buddy dance," I said.

"Go," said Joel. "Live a little."

"Harrison, you should go," said my mother. "You like Anna and she'll take you."

"If you do go, what are you going to wear, Bud?" Joel asked.

"If I do go," I said, "and I might not, I was thinking of black pants and a grey t-shirt because the dance is scheduled for a Thursday." I picked up my fork.

"It's a Halloween dance," said Joel. "You have to wear a costume."

"It's okay, Harrison," said my mother, "you don't have to dress up. Just the fact that you might go would be a big step, even if you only stay for half an hour. I think you should attempt this social event."

Normally, dressing up meant I had to wear a white shirt and a tie and I had to do that when I went to church or a function with my father.

"I wasn't planning on wearing a tie," I said.

"When I said dress up," said my mother, "I meant in a costume."

"I bet Anna wears a costume," said Joel.

"Pass the salad," said my father. Joel picked up the bowl and passed it to my father. I didn't look at it. Or look at the lasagne. It had tomatoes in it and cheese and pasta.

"I agree with your mother," said my father. "Just go for half an hour or even twenty minutes. I wasn't into dances at your age either but I remember going to one and having a blast."

"A blast, Dad? Really. Wow." Joel stuffed food in his mouth.

"Maybe I should talk to Anna," said my mother.

My hands started flapping so I sat on them and stared down at my plate with chicken, rice, and beans. Nothing was touching.

"Harrison, you don't have to wear a costume," said my father.

"I need to think about this," I said.

After dinner I went to my room to do homework: math and English. I liked math but not English and I wasn't going to do the English tonight because I didn't want to. I would do the math. Tomorrow I would have to see a special teacher for the English because I didn't want to do it even though everyone thought I should. The story we were supposed to read made no sense. It was about a monkey's paw but that's not what the teacher wanted me to think it was about. When my special teacher asked me about it I said it was about a monkey's paw. Then she asked me to read more into it and I said there was nothing to read into it. It was about a monkey's paw. She said it had underlying themes but I thought it should have been only about a monkey's paw.

Math was easier. A knock rapped on my door.

"Harrison," said my mother.

"Yes."

"Can I come in?"

"Yes."

She opened the door and walked over to my desk. "How's English?"

"I'm not going to do my English homework tonight."

"Why not?"

"I don't like the story. But I'll do my math."

She exhaled. "I'll work on the story with you."

"No," I said. "It's about a monkey's paw but it's not really, and that doesn't make sense."

"Perhaps we should discuss this with your teacher." She exhaled, and the sound was loud. "Now about the Halloween party. You don't have to wear a costume."

"I know." I'm not sure why she came to my room to tell me that.

I did my math homework until exactly 9:00 pm. Then I went to the kitchen to have a bowl of Special K with milk. I ate the same snack every night. Joel was in the kitchen eating nachos and cheese with salsa. Today, he didn't have friends over so he wasn't double dipping. His hair was wet from his hockey practice.

"Do you wear flip flops when you shower?" I asked him. "If you don't you could get foot fungus."

"Hi, to you too," he said. "And the answer is no. No flip flops." He stuck his bare feet in the air.

"Foot fungus is contagious," I said.

"Isn't it time for your Special K?"

"Yes. And that is why I'm now in the kitchen."

Joel crunched on his corn chips while I got the box of Special K out of the pantry. The box was almost empty so I put Special K on Mom's grocery list.

"If you want," said Joel when I sat down with a bowl and milk, "I can help you find a cool costume."

"I don't want to wear a costume."

"Girls like it when guys wear costumes. It's more fun."

I lowered my head and ate my cereal.

There were no red bicycles on the street today so I sat in the front seat. "Today, after I enter the Science Centre, I will have been there 889 times," I said to my mother.

"I think I know that," replied my mother. "Did Anna say she would meet you out front?"

"Yes."

"Remember to be appropriate. No peeing outside on a tree."

"I won't drink soda."

"Maybe you and Anna could do something else besides the Science Centre. Why don't *you* suggest your next meeting be somewhere different?"

She pulled up in front of the Science Centre. "There's Anna," she said.

I glanced out the window and saw her standing by the entrance, wearing flat shoes.

"I will pick you up in two hours," said my mom. "Have fun. And remember to try to look her in the eyes at least once."

I got out of the car and walked over to Anna. "This will be my 889th time at the Science Centre," I said. "I like the number nine but when I get to my 895th time I'll just walk in and walk out because I don't like the number five."

"Oh," said Anna. "What happened when you got to 500?"

"I went in and out 100 times. It took me 57 minutes."

"It must have been expensive to buy that many tickets all at once."

"I had a season's pass."

"Good thing," she said. She handed me a ticket that she must have purchased while she was waiting for me to arrive.

"I don't have a season's pass this year because my parents thought I would be too busy with high school. I only do math homework. We had to read a story about a monkey's paw but it wasn't really about a paw."

"That is a tough story to understand," she said. "Homework is a killer in high school."

"I'm not sure I agree with that," I said. "It hasn't killed me because I'm here right now."

She laughed and I liked it when she laughed because her voice sounded nice.

After one hour and fifty-nine minutes at the Science Centre I took off my headset. Anna did too and came over to me right away. "I have an idea," she said.

"Let's eat in the cafeteria," I said. I didn't want to hear that she wanted to go to a restaurant down the street with a red awning.

"Sure," she said. "But first let's go to the gift store."

"I like the gift store," I said.

"Oh good," she said. "What if we found you something really cool from the gift store to wear to the Halloween dance?"

"Once I dressed up for Halloween in a costume," I said as we walked to the gift store. "I wore a Superman cape and went out with Joel. I got tired and didn't want to go to the house but Joel did because they gave out good candy. When Joel was at a house getting candy, two boys pulled my cape over my face and took my orange plastic bucket. I couldn't see. I had a meltdown on the street."

"That's awful," said Anna.

"My mom doesn't like my meltdowns either."

"I meant it was awful those kids stole your candy and ruined Halloween for you," she said. "This will be a fun Halloween for you and you don't have to wear a cape. Maybe we can find a cool shirt with bones on it."

I thought about wearing a t-shirt with bones on it and that made me happy. My hands didn't flap. "Okay," I said. "But we might have to take the tag out. I don't like shirts with tags."

"That's doable," she said.

"My mother sews soft coverings on my shirts after she takes the tags out."

"Smart mother," she said.

The gift store sold all kinds of things and when I was little my mother would buy me things, until one day she told me we couldn't buy something every time we went to the Science

Centre because we went so often. "I haven't been in the gift store in a long time," I said.

Anna walked right over to a rack that had t-shirts so I followed her. She took a hanger off the rack and held up a long-sleeved t-shirt for me to see. "Look at this one," she said.

All of the bones of the ribcage and the clavicle and the arm bones were printed on a black background. It was like the front of a skeleton but only the upper body. Then she turned the shirt around and it showed the skeleton from the back.

"Wow," I said. "I've never seen a shirt like that before." And I hadn't.

"Do you like it?" she asked.

"Yes," I said. I reached out to touch it.

"I was thinking that perhaps you could wear it as a costume to the Halloween dance. I'd really like you to come with me."

"My brother said I should go to the dance. So did my mother and father. And my friend, Alan."

"What if there were some activity tables so you didn't have to just dance?" Anna asked. "Tables where you could build things?"

I thought about this. "Maybe if there was a Lego table it would be okay. Or a table with video games like *First Responders*."

"Those are great suggestions," said Anna.

Since I was supposed to look her in the eyes once every time we met, I glanced at her. She was smiling. I smiled back.

"I want a hot dog now," I said. "In the cafeteria."

When my mother picked me up and I got in the front seat of the car she asked, "What's in the bag?"

"Anna bought me a shirt and it is going to be my costume for the Halloween dance. And I looked her in the eye once."

"Harrison, that's fantastic," she said. As she pulled away from the curb, she asked, "Does that mean you are going to the dance? Can I see the shirt?"

"Not when you're driving. It would be distracting for you. And that is two questions at once."

"Okay, well maybe you can tell me what it looks like."

At the stop light where it was red and we had to wait in an idle position, I explained the shirt. I told my mother how it looked like a skeleton and that it was black and white, no colours, and how I liked it because I liked bones.

"That Anna is a clever girl," she said. She put on her blinker and moved over a lane to pass a car.

I checked the speedometer. "You're going too fast."

She slowed down. "I was thinking about inviting Anna over for dinner one night. What do you think about that idea?"

I checked the speedometer and when I saw she was going the speed limit I said, "I think it's a good idea. I will phone her."

# CHAPTER TEN
## ANNA

The Science Centre gift store is located on the main floor beside the cafeteria. I went in to the gift store, thinking that maybe it would have something for Harrison's Halloween costume. I browsed through the hats first and found one that looked like a brain but I wondered if a hat might be too much for him. A hat on his head might be uncomfortable. For some reason it didn't seem right. Next I rifled through the shirts.

When I found one with a skeleton on it, I yanked it off the hanger and laughed out loud. He just might like this one. It was a t-shirt, and he wore t-shirts all the time. Fingers crossed. And it was a medium men's too. Perfect. I shoved it in with the smalls and put it at the back of the rack so it would be easy to find later, if I could get him into the gift shop.

For the entire time we were in the Science Centre exhibits, I kept thinking about the shirt. After all, we were at the same exhibit on the human body, and since I'd gone through all the displays last time, I wasn't that keen on going through them again. Harrison had been through them 889 times. Good God.

As soon as I saw him take off his head set, I raced over to him. Now for the challenge of getting him into the gift store.

"Let's eat in the cafeteria," he said.

"Sure," I said. Yup, my idea to go to a cute little café had thoroughly tanked. "But let's go to the gift store first."

"I like the gift store," he said.

"Oh, good," I said, eyeing him. "What if we found you something really cool from the gift store to wear to the Halloween dance?"

"Once I dressed up for Halloween in a costume," he said as we walked to the gift store. "I wore a Superman cape and went out with Joel. I got tired and didn't want to go to the house but Joel did because they gave out good candy. When Joel was at a house getting candy, two boys pulled my cape over my face and took my orange plastic bucket. I couldn't see. I had a meltdown on the street."

"That's awful," I said. Why did kids have to be so mean? And why did some kids have it worse than others?

"My mom doesn't like my meltdowns either."

"I meant it was awful those kids stole your candy and ruined Halloween for you," I said. I had to make him see that Halloween could be fun. No one would be mean to him at the Best Buddies dance. "This will be a fun Halloween for you," I said, "and you don't have to wear a cape. Maybe we can find a cool shirt with bones on it."

"Okay," he said.

I couldn't wait to show him the shirt and I crossed my fingers, hoping it was still where I'd stashed it. When I saw it, I grinned. "Look at this one," I said.

"Wow," he said with more enthusiasm than I'd ever heard in his voice. "I've never seen a shirt like that before."

"Do you like it?" I asked. From his voice I thought he did

but I wanted to hear him say it.

"Yes," he said. Then he reached out and touched it.

As I watched him touch it, almost reverently, my heart was ready to burst.

"I was thinking," I said, "that perhaps you could wear it as a costume to the Halloween dance. I'd really like you to come with me."

"My brother said I should go to the dance. So did my mother and father. And my friend, Alan."

"What if there were some activity tables so you didn't have to just dance?" I asked. "Tables where you could build things?"

He tilted his head and I knew he was thinking. This was good. He didn't say no. And he wasn't flapping his hands. "Maybe," he said, "if there was a Lego table it would be okay. Or a table with video games like *First Responders*."

I clapped my hands. "Those are great suggestions!" If I could have hugged him, I would have. I was definitely making progress.

Then he glanced at me and for a moment, he really looked me in the eyes. Like really looked me in the eyes. And he smiled. I grinned back because I just couldn't help it.

"I want a hot dog now," he said. "In the cafeteria."

I laughed. "Come on," I said. "Let's go."

"Why would you make that stupid chicken dance song your ringtone? Hurry up and answer it, for God's sake," Marnie squealed. We were at the mall, shopping for clothes. Marnie was convinced I needed a new outfit for my date with Justin, which was tonight.

I laughed. "I like it — it's corny and fun. Plus I put it on to bug my mother because she is so *not* fun. It drives her crazy every time my phone rings. And I never answer until at least four rings."

"Answer it! That's been at least four!"

"Three," I corrected. I pulled my phone out of my purse and when I saw it was the Henrys' number, I clicked answer. "Hello?"

"Anna, this is Harrison Henry."

"Harrison!" I glanced over at Marnie and gave her my shocked raised-eyebrows look. Harrison never called me, ever. I always called him.

"My mother was wondering if you would like to have dinner at our house on Wednesday night."

"I would love to," I answered.

"If you could be here at 6:00 o'clock that would be best."

"I will be there at 6:00," I said. "Thank you for asking me." I pressed end and held up my thumb.

"Harrison?" Marnie asked.

"I'm making progress," I said. "He just asked me over for dinner at his house."

"Ooh-la-la. Is the *brother* going to be there? Oh, did I tell you I know someone who plays on his hockey team? I'm going to their next game. I hope he introduces me."

"I haven't met him yet."

"Would you get on that? For me? Your *best friend*." Marnie made a pretend pout. "I wish I could go to dinner with you. My parents are making me go to that College Fair on at the community Centre. They're so afraid I'm not getting in anywhere. I wish they'd let up and let me do it on my own."

Uh oh. I had totally forgotten about that event. I pulled my phone out of my pocket and went to my schedule icon. I had forgotten to even put it in my phone.

"I'm surprised you're not going," said Marnie.

"Oh crap, Marnie. When my mother finds out I've made other plans she is going to go ballistic."

"Why do you need to go? With your grades you'll get in anywhere you apply. I'm sure you've got all the schools you want picked out anyway. That's you."

"Exactly," I said. "But try telling my mom that."

Marnie pointed to a window mannequin. "Now that's an outfit that would look good on you. Come on." She grabbed my arm and marched us both into the store.

Dressed in my new outfit that consisted of a short jean skirt, an oversized funky maroon t-shirt, and a pair of black shortie boots with three inch heels, I went downstairs.

"Mom!"

No answer. Of course, my mother wasn't home so there was no one to say 'you look good,' or 'where are you off to?' or even just 'goodbye.' I rarely wore heels but Marnie convinced me to buy them because they made my legs look good. I also thought the outfit would be great to flaunt in front of my mother — strut through the kitchen and make her say something snarky or, better yet, ask where I was going. Maybe then she would notice me for something other than my grades.

But of course, she ruined my plan by not being home.

When I pulled up in front of Justin's house, he was outside waiting for me and I have to admit I was a little disappointed. I wanted to knock on the door, be invited in, and meet his family. Maybe even his sister. It seemed he kept her close to his heart but out of sight.

Before I could even say hi, he said, "I'm so sorry you have to drive." He shook his head. "One more month." He held up his first finger. "And I get my car back."

"I don't care," I said, glancing in my rear view and side mirror before pulling away from the curb.

"But I do," he said. "My dad is being a jerk."

"What is he punishing you for?"

"Something that happened at my last school."

"What?" I said, eyeing him sideways.

"I got in a fight. Other than that, it's not worth the words to tell you," he said casually. "So, this movie is supposed to be awesome. It's based on a true story about a guy who got caught in an avalanche and survived."

"Yeah, I read all the reviews. It looks good."

"I know I ask this all the time, but how's Harrison?"

"Oh," I said with excitement. "He invited me to dinner on Wednesday night. I really think I'm making progress."

"Good for you," he said.

We didn't talk for a few moments. Then he leaned over, touched my cheek and said, "You look great tonight."

My entire body tingled under his touch and I thought I was going to drive off the road.

On Wednesday, for my dinner at Harrison's, I decided to wear my new shirt but with a pair of jeans. The short skirt might give Harrison's family the wrong impression. Marnie told me my new boots would look good with my jeans and I had to agree after I tried on the outfit in my bedroom. Nerves were overtaking me: my stomach rolled and my palms were sweating.

"Breathe, Anna, breathe," I said to myself as I slung my purse over my shoulder.

Surprise, surprise — my mother was in the kitchen, drinking coffee. She looked at me over the rim of her reading glasses. "You look nice," she said.

"Thanks."

"It's important to make a good impression."

"I know."

"Don't waste time on schools you definitely aren't going to. Like Queens. Just go right to the booths for Princeton, Yale, and Harvard and shake hands and make small talk."

"I'm, uh, not going to the College Fair," I mumbled.

"Why not? This is important. You never know —"

"— who you can meet." I finished. "I know, Mom, you've told me that a million times before. I've been invited to Harrison's for dinner."

"Dinner? I thought joining this club was just to build your resume. So you can make a good impression at a *College Fair*. Dinner at someone's house is personal."

"He invited me and I said yes."

"You could have said you were busy or that you would rather stick to structured meetings."

"That would sound pretty cold, Mom."

She held up her hands. "I think you're getting too

involved but, hey, this is your deal. But if all these "meetings" start to impede your marks then you should think twice about the program. Remember, it is about resume building. And your future."

"OMG. He is a *real* person, you know. And he's important to me."

"And real doctors don't have personal relationships with patients."

"I'm not a doctor yet."

She cleared her throat and exhaled. Yup, she was exasperated. That was her sign. She did it in court all the time. I turned to leave.

"How is your essay coming along for your early admission to Princeton?" she asked before I managed to get out the door. My body tensed. There was no way I was going to turn around and face her.

"You want me to proofread it?"

"No, that's okay. I should get going." I jingled my keys.

"You are working on the essay, correct? And the application?"

"Stop bugging me about this."

"Anna, if this program is taking too much of your time and you are not getting your work done then you should reconsider."

Her words made me do an about face. I glared at her. "I'm not quitting him," I snapped. "What about your whole philosophy *that hard work gets things done?*"

"What you're doing is not exactly hard work, sweetie. It's more like…babysitting."

"I can't believe you just said that!" I could feel my blood

heating up. My cheeks flushed. "But I guess I can," I had to continue. "It's kind of like how you quit on me, on Anna the human being, once I was born. All I've ever been is some prodigy kid to you."

"That is not true," she stepped towards me.

"It is so true." I ran out of the house, slamming the door on the way out. I could hear her calling my name but I raced to my car and flung open the door. My hands shook as I started the engine and I could feel the tears pooling behind my eyes. I peeled away from the curb, banging my hands on the steering wheel.

By the time I got to Harrison's my face was streaked with mascara and I looked like crap. Sitting in the car, I pulled the visor down, wiped my eyes, fluffed up my hair, and put on a little lip gloss. Almost involuntarily my body heaved out this huge sigh. I wanted to do this no matter what my stupid mother said. School was important, yes, but so was the real world. For once in my life I felt as if I was *really* accomplishing something.

Still trying to compose myself, I walked slowly up the sidewalk to the front door. I went up the steps and stood at the door for a second. And another second. And another. Then I knocked.

Harrison answered as if he had been standing behind the door waiting for me. "Hello, Anna," he said.

"Hi Harrison." I smiled at him. He made me smile. Forget about my mother.

He ushered me in. "There are twenty-six bones in the feet," he said, his voice high. "That means that there are fifty-two bones in both feet. High heels hurt the bones of the feet, in particular the navicular, cuboid, and cuneiform. There are three parts to the cuneiform."

I didn't know if I should interrupt his reciting bones or not. I decided not to and bent over and unzipped my new boots. The high note in his voice was not a good sign.

"Harrison," said his mother who appeared from around the corner. "Introduce me to Anna."

"There are twenty-six bones of the feet." His words were coming out like they were being spit out like sunflower seed shells. "That means there are fifty-two bones in both feet." His speech was getting faster and faster with every word.

Okay. Obviously he was upset about something.

His mother smiled at me, but it was a superficial face-smile, and I could see the tension behind it. "Anna, it's nice to finally meet you face to face."

"Nice to meet you," I said. I lined up my boots because I knew that was probably important to Harrison. Harrison's voice, reciting the bones of the feet, got louder and louder.

When I stood back up, his hands were flapping.

"Harrison," said his mother. "Breathe, okay? Just breathe."

He really did try, but it didn't seem to work. His agitation seemed to be escalating. Then his mother called out, "Joel!"

I felt as if I was rooted to my spot and couldn't move. If I stepped toward him he might get worse. My stomach plummeted and I wanted to cry, again, for the second time in one evening. Joel appeared from around the corner. "What's up?" When he saw Harrison he said, "Whoa. Breathe, Bud, breathe."

"I'm going to try and get him to his room," said Harrison's mother to Joel. "Could you take Anna to the family room and get her something to drink?"

"I'm okay," I said, hurriedly. "I don't need a drink."

"Come on, Harrison," said his mother. "Maybe we should go to your room."

Flapping like a freaked-out hummingbird, Harrison did what he was told, leaving me with Joel.

"Hey," he said. "I'm Joel." He stuck out his hand and I shook it.

"Anna," I said. "I'm so sorry. I don't know what I did to upset him. I feel horrible. We'd been making such good progress together."

Joel looked down at the floor and pointed to my shoes. "Ahhh. High heels. They can set him off."

"High heels?" Then I remembered my first conversation with him and how he had asked me if I had worn high heels.

"I didn't know that," I said.

"*Someone* should have told you. Or, he should just get over it." He jerked his head toward the place where he had come from and even that little gesture made him look cool and so unbelievably good looking. It was no wonder that Marnie wanted to hook up with him. "I have my orders," he said. "We need to go to the family room."

In my sock feet, I followed him to a room with a big television, plush comfortable sofas, a recliner, a coffee table, and loads of family photos on the wall. It looked comfortable, inviting. We had a family room but it was full of law and business books.

"Have a seat," said Joel. He flopped down on the big sofa and I chose to sit on the love seat. "How come someone like you isn't at the College Fair?"

"I've got the three schools picked that I want to go to."

"Oh yeah? Which ones?"

"Queens. And University of California, Berkeley. And Los Angeles. What about you? How come you didn't go?"

"I have a hockey scholarship at University of Minnesota, so ditto. I know where I'm going. Do you like hockey?" he asked, pointing to the game on the television.

I shrugged. "Sort of."

We didn't talk for a few moments and I tried to listen for Harrison's voice, to see if he was still reciting.

Joel glanced over at me. "He'll be okay," he said. "It's getting quieter up there. My mom *might* be able to deal with him."

"I hope so," I said. "I feel horrible that I set him off."

"It's not your fault. It's not the first time and it won't be the last. But he is getting better. I think the program has helped him. You've been good for him."

My cheeks burned. I needed to hear that tonight after the altercation with my mother, but having it come from one of the most popular boys in school made me feel awkward. We sat in silence for a few moments and there was no noise from upstairs.

I picked up a photo from the side table and stared at it. Harrison looked to be around five and Joel seven. "What was he like when he was little?"

"Kind of what he is like now, only he had way more meltdowns. Sometimes he would just flop down in the middle of Walmart and go at it. My mom called it flailing. Sometimes his shoes would fly off his feet. My job was to pick them up."

"That must have been hard."

"We've all been to therapy to learn how to deal with him.

It's helped. He just obsesses over things and he doesn't have a practical bone in his body, which of course is a funny thing to say, seeing as he is *fixated* on bones. My parents kept telling me that he processes things differently. And when he can't process, he flaps or walks in circles to help. The walking in circles has just started."

"I saw him do that the other day," I said.

"Sometimes he can go for an hour. It's exhausting to watch. But it does help him cope, I guess. He might grow out of it."

"Has he always obsessed over the human body?"

"That's been a few years. For a while when he was little, it was Pokemon. Even when it wasn't cool." He rolled his eyes. "And Lego. He still plays with Lego but now he builds amazing stuff with it, like robots, so that is totally on the radar. But he has obsessed over germs his entire life. I used to have to step on a towel if I went into his room. Finally my parents made him get over the towel thing."

"Did he ever play any sports?" I asked. "Do any activities?"

Joel laughed. "Harrison? Sports? Have you watched him throw a ball? He is really uncoordinated. I used to dress him up as a goalie and take shots on him. Then one day the puck hit him in the head and he had a huge meltdown. He never put the equipment on again."

"Poor kid."

"Yeah. It was too bad for both of us." Joel sat forward and stared at the television. "Skate," he yelled.

"Darn, they hit the post," he said when there was no goal. He leaned back again and turned to me. "Oh and FYI, besides high heels, he doesn't do well with perfume."

"Thank goodness I didn't wear perfume today," I said. "I had thought about it but then I forgot when I was deciding on what shoes to wear. So at least I got it half right."

A door slammed and the noise made me jump. "Don't worry," said Joel. "My dad is home from work. I better go help in the kitchen." He hopped over the sofa.

"I can help too," I said, following him around the sofa.

"A friend of mine has a friend on your hockey team," I said to Joel, trying to make conversation as we walked to the kitchen, plus Marnie would never forgive me if I didn't mention her. "She was thinking of going to your next game. You play on Thursday, right?"

"Home opener," said Joel.

"She says you're one of the best on the team."

"I'm okay." He gave a cool shrug.

"Wow, you're being modest."

He turned and grinned at me. "Would you mind saying that a little louder when we walk into the kitchen? I'd love to see my mother's face."

"Not a chance." I laughed just as we entered the kitchen, a large room with a big window overlooking a backyard that now had flower beds with fading autumn blooms. I was surprised to see Harrison placing plates on the table. He didn't look at me or Joel. Mr. Henry was undoing the knot in his tie and Mrs. Henry was stirring something at the stove.

"Hi, Harrison," I said as casually as I could.

"You're laughing," he said.

"Just at something Joel said about hockey," I said.

Harrison seemed to be okay with that and returned to setting the table. From what I could see he was doing a fantastic job at lining up the plates perfectly.

Mrs. Henry turned and gave me a reassuring smile, so I was able to relax a bit. There seemed to be a normal family routine to the situation now. Everything was going to be fine.

"Anna, meet Harrison's father, Bill."

"Hi," I said, extending my hand. "Pleased to meet you."

He shook it and also smiled at me, this genuine, kind smile. "We're so glad you're joining us."

"Thank you for inviting me," I replied. "It smells really good in here," I said. "A homemade meal will be a treat." Thoughts of my mother knifed through me.

"I invited her," said Harrison, and his voice was a little elevated. I turned to gaze at him. "I made the phone call," he said.

"Yes, you did," said Mrs. Henry in this super soft voice. "Breathe, Harrison."

I looked at Harrison and could see agitation creeping into him again. Now he was holding silverware in his hands. "I really appreciate you asking me, Harrison," I said. He seemed to calm a bit. I wanted his family to know I cared so I said, "I can help you set the table."

"No," he stated. "I set the table every day and I make twenty-one dollars a week."

"Harrison," said his father. "Breathe."

His hands started flapping and silverware clanged to the floor. I stepped back and glanced at Joel. He was running his hands through his hair and shaking his head as if he knew the situation was out of his control.

Mr. Henry stood in front of Harrison and talked quietly to him. "You can do this, Harrison."

"She wore high heels. There are twenty-six bones in the feet. High heels hurt the bones in the feet. Anna and Joel were laughing." He flapped his hands and shook his head back and forth like a dog playing tug of war. If he didn't slow down he was going to get whiplash.

When his father stepped away from him, a feeling of doom settled in the room. My heart raced and I swear I could feel my blood pumping.

"He's going to flail," said his mother.

I stepped back and watched as Harrison threw himself on the floor in a full-blown tantrum.

# CHAPTER ELEVEN
## HARRISON

When I was putting my fourth plate on the table, Joel and Anna walked in the kitchen and she was laughing. Why were they laughing together? I didn't want them to laugh together. If I was her boyfriend, she should laugh with me. And I didn't want them laughing *at me*. I put the last plate down. My mother had made me calm down upstairs and she told me to forget about the high heels. I felt okay but knew I was still spinning inside my head and I was trying to not let that happen.

"Hi, Harrison," said Anna.

"You're laughing," I said.

"Just at something Joel said about hockey," she said.

Since I was finished with the plates, I picked up the silverware. I set the table the same way every day. Plates first, then forks, knives, and spoons and at the very end I put a paper serviette beside every plate. I picked up five forks. I needed to concentrate on setting the table and that would help me to stop the spinning.

My mother was stirring something at the stove, something I wasn't going to eat because it was a soup and I didn't like soup. My dad was home but I don't know what time he got home and that bothered me. On the weekends, he cooked, and during the week, my mother cooked. My mother had taken me to my room so I couldn't see Anna's high heels and I had missed my dad coming in the back door.

"Anna," said my mother, "meet Harrison's father, Bill."

"Hi," Anna said. "Pleased to meet you."

I lined up another fork.

"We're so glad you're joining us," said my father.

"Thank you for inviting me," she replied.

He didn't invite her, I did. I phoned her cell phone and asked for her and invited her to come to dinner at my house. Why did she think *he* had invited her?

"I invited her," I yelled so everyone would know that I made the call to her cell phone and asked her to dinner. "I made the phone call," I said. Everyone was always trying to get me to do things and then when I did them, they didn't think I did.

"Yes, you did," said my mother. "Breathe, Harrison."

Why was she telling me to breathe? My hands weren't flapping yet. Why didn't they know that I had made the phone call? Boys called girls and that's what I had done, just like all the teens on television and like Joel.

"I really appreciate you asking me, Harrison," said Anna.

It made me feel better that she knew that I had asked her. I was now finished with the forks and I picked up the knives.

"I can help you set the table," she said.

If she helped me set the table would I have to share my money with her? I made twenty-one dollars a week, and that meant three dollars per meal. If I shared the duty with her, would I have to pay her half of three dollars, which was $1.50? Maybe it wouldn't be that much though because so far she hadn't helped with the plates or the forks and was only going to help with the knives. I would have to divide twenty into twenty-one because twenty would be the amount of plates, forks, knives and spoons that had to be put on the table. Twenty didn't go into twenty-one.

*Twenty didn't go into twenty-one.*

Words started spinning in my head: plates, knives, forks, spoons, twenty, twenty-one. I tried to breathe. In through the nose and out through the mouth. *Breathe, breathe.*

"No!" I managed to say. This was good; I was able to talk. "I set the table every day and I make twenty-one dollars a week."

"Harrison," said my father. "Breathe."

I *was* breathing. I had been breathing on my own. Why did he have to tell me? I was doing it on my own until he started telling me. Why wouldn't they just let me do it on my own? Words spun. Around and around. They kept spinning. Now I did need to breathe but I couldn't. My father had ruined it for me.

My hands started flapping and all the silverware I had in my hands clanged to the floor. The noise was so loud in my brain it hurt, and resounded from side to side. I flapped my hands hoping to get rid of the sound in my head of knives hitting the floor.

My dad stood in front of me. "You can do this, Harrison." His loud voice hit the side wall of my brain too and now it was mixed with the sound of the silverware clinking. Why did he have to talk in such a loud voice? I wanted to walk in circles but there wasn't room to walk in circles with so many people in the kitchen. I saw Anna's feet. She had socks on and not high heels but I could still see her high heels in my brain and they were boots and black and they would hurt her feet.

"She wore high heels. There are twenty-six bones in the feet. High heels hurt the bones in the feet." If I recited the bones I might be able to stop the spinning. I had to walk in circles. Three steps. And around. My foot landed on a knife. The noise got stuck in my head. I hated loud noises. They hurt me. Hurt my head. I could also hear Anna and Joel laughing.

"Anna and Joel were laughing," I said.

My hands just wouldn't stop flapping. I shook my head back and forth to get rid of the noises. Back and forth. Back and forth. Too many noises. No room to walk. I felt the explosion coming, racing from my head to my hands and legs. Soon, nothing would work. I wouldn't be able to stand up.

I fell to the floor to get the words and noises out of my brain. I moved my arms and legs, just wanting everything gone. I kept flailing.

When my brain was emptied, I lay on the floor. I was tired. My mom leaned over me. "Harrison," she said. "Let's go to your room for a little bit."

I got up off the floor and walked to my room, shut the door, and pulled out my Lego bin. *Snap. Snap. Snap.* I put the pieces together. I would build the most amazing robot. My mother left me alone. I liked being alone in my room; it was my safe place.

My robot grew and grew. I snapped on another piece of Lego to make it bigger. I wanted it to have three Jedi levels instead of one. I didn't like that I had a meltdown when we were supposed to eat dinner at my house, with my mom cooking, and my dad and Joel home, and Anna sitting at the table too. It made my stomach hurt.

Downstairs, in the kitchen, I could hear them talking

and the noise of silverware on plates. My mother had made a special Thai meal: coconut soup and rice and a special dish that had vegetables and chicken and nuts. I would have had chicken and rice and beans because I don't like my food mixing but I was in my room building a Lego robot. And Anna was downstairs in my house eating dinner.

Anna was my friend and I wanted to be at dinner but she had worn high heels to my house. And she had laughed with Joel. I didn't want her to be Joel's girlfriend. I wanted her to be my girlfriend and go to the dance with me, not Joel. What if she went to the dance with Joel? I had a new t-shirt that I was supposed to wear and my mom had already washed it and put soft tags on it and I wanted to wear it to the dance. If she went with Joel then she couldn't go with me and I couldn't wear my t-shirt. I wanted to go to the dance with her but I didn't want to kiss her. Kissing was trading saliva, which meant trading germs. I didn't want to get a bacterial infection or a virus or mononucleosis.

Someone knocked on my door. "Harrison," said my mom.

I didn't answer.

She opened my door. "Anna is leaving now," she said. "Would you like to say goodbye?"

"Is that appropriate?" I asked without looking at my mother.

"Yes," she replied.

I stood up and walked over to the door.

"You'll be fine," said my mom.

Anna was still in the kitchen and she was clearing plates from the table, and taking them to the sink. She had her back turned to me and was in sock feet. I didn't get paid to clear plates so it was fine that she helped.

"Anna," said my mother.

She turned and smiled. I lowered my head. I couldn't look her in the eyes even though I liked it when she smiled at me. "Hi, Harrison," she said.

"Hello, Anna."

"Thank you for inviting me to dinner," she said.

"You're welcome."

"I'm going to head home now though. I have a lot of homework to do."

"I have homework too," I said.

"What subjects?"

"Math and English. I don't like English. I don't like writing essays."

"If you ever need help, let me know," said Anna.

"I have special teachers," I said. "Are you going to put on your high heels when you leave?"

"How about I carry them to my car? Then you won't have to see them."

"I think it would be better if we said goodbye in the kitchen."

"That's a great idea," she said.

Her voice sounded nice and I liked it when she said that I had a great idea. I lifted my head a little and looked at her out of the corner of my eyes. I would tell Alan she was pretty and nice. My mother told me I was always supposed to say thank you at the end of things. "Thank you for coming, Anna."

She laughed and I liked the sound and how it tinkled and it made me feel good inside because she was laughing with me and not Joel.

"It was my pleasure," she said.

On the way to school the next day, driving with my mother and not Joel, I thought a lot about Anna. My mother had talked to me last night and Joel too, and she told me if I was going to have friends I couldn't have big meltdowns anymore. They both thought I should go back to the therapist and get more coping techniques. I didn't like Stella, my therapist, and I told my mother that and after she put her finger to the middle of her forehead she said she would look for a new one but we had gone through a lot of them already.

Sitting in the car, thinking of Stella and what had happened with Anna made me flap. I sat on my hands so my mother wouldn't see. I had wanted to sit in the back but she said I had to sit in the front.

Phys ed was my first class and it was one of my worst subjects. I was never good at it, even in elementary school. Today we were square dancing and that meant everyone had to have a partner. Since the teachers weren't picking, I ended up with a boy with bad body odour.

"You should wear deodorant," I said to him.

"And you should shut your trap," he replied.

We didn't have to touch each other because I was known as the boy with autism. For once I was happy about that because I think I might have had a big meltdown if I'd have touched the boy with the bad body odour, and my mom and Joel told me I wasn't supposed to have meltdowns now that I was older.

I couldn't move my feet the way the teachers were telling

me to and they seemed to get all mixed up and I almost fell into the boy with the bad body odour.

"Watch it," he said. Then he called to the teacher. "Mrs. Callan. I can't dance with this dork."

I breathed in through my nose and out through my mouth. I didn't like being called a dork.

"Harrison, let me show you."

I tried to follow her feet and her arms, but I never did get the hang of it. The class ended and all I could think about was what a bad dancer I was and how at the Halloween dance I was going to have to dance with Anna. The teens in the television show hadn't danced like we just did in phys ed. What if they put on square-dancing music at the dance and I had to dance like that and I almost fell on Anna like I did with the boy with body odour? She wasn't very tall and I might knock her over. I hoped she didn't wear high heels to the dance. I shook my head. I would have to tell her not to.

With my head down, I walked to my next class. So many words were bouncing around in my head, like *Anna* and *dance* and *square dancing*. Then the music from phys ed started playing in my head and it started getting louder and louder with each step I took. I could also hear my feet clomping on the floor and the sounds of kids running down the hall and talking and whispering and laughing. I put my hands to my head and kept walking, staring down at the tiles, counting them. The lines were jumping out at me. Why were they doing that? Usually I only had problems with going through doors. But the lines on the floor were bouncing and jumping. I stopped and tapped my foot over a line. I would have to dodge them. Not step on them. Why were they doing this? I didn't like this. I didn't want them to do this. It was all because of the music.

Someone bumped into me.

"Watch where you're going, Dork!" I recognized the voice. It was a boy I had gone to elementary school with and he was the one who named Alan and me Dork and Pork.

"What happened to your friend Pork?" He laughed.

The sound of his voice was loud and it got stuck with the square-dancing music. His name was Kyle and in elementary school he pushed me and took my lunch. Once, I had a huge meltdown after he took my lunch and everyone called me Spazz after that. Spazzy Dork. I put my hands to my ears to stop the noise. I didn't want him to take my lunch. I had a ham sandwich and I liked ham sandwiches because they were like hot dogs.

"Grab his backpack," Kyle said.

Someone pushed me down and someone else sat on me and ripped my arms back and took my backpack off my shoulders. Pain shot through my arms. "Don't take my lunch," I said. "I have a ham sandwich. I have to get to class. I'm going to be late." My hands were trying to flap. "I can't be late."

"Look at him," Kyle taunted. "He's flapping like a baby seal." Kyle made a loud honking noise that hurt my ears. I tried to stand up and someone pushed me down. I felt a kick to my ribs.

"A human rib cage has two sets of twenty-four ribs," I gasped. Then someone kicked my leg. "There are two bones in the lower leg," I said. "The tibia and fibula."

I had to say the bones or I might have a meltdown. I didn't want to have a meltdown in the hallway at school. My mother and Joel told me to stop having meltdowns. If I had one, I would have to go to the office and not eat my ham sandwich and not go to class, or I would have to walk in late and everyone would stare at me and call me Dork. Spazzy Dork. I didn't want to be late. If I could get up I could walk in circles. Three steps. Round the corner. I had to get up and walk in circles.

"What are you guys doing?" a voice screamed.

Noise. Noise. Noise. Kids yelled. Lockers clanged. The noise reverberated in my head. I flapped and flapped and flapped and tried not to listen.

# CHAPTER TWELVE
## ANNA

Lead feet. Heavy heart. I walked to my next class feeling like a sorry failure. Yesterday had been a complete disaster with my mother and Harrison, and now today I found out I'd only received 85% on my English essay. My mother would shake her head at me if she found out and she would blame it all on Harrison. Last night when I had got home from Harrison's, she had been up and wanted to talk about what I'd said to her but I said I was tired and didn't want to talk. Maybe I should take her up on her suggestion to quit the program. Obviously, judging by last night's disaster, I was *not* making progress and it *was* causing my marks to suffer.

"What are you guys doing?" I heard Justin's voice coming from around the corner. "Leave him alone!"

The anger in his voice freaked me out. Then I heard a loud clanging noise like a kid had been pushed against a locker. Students were really yelling now. What was going on?

"Fight!"

Oh, God, he couldn't be in another fight.

I ran down the hall, pushing bodies out of the way without saying excuse me. One girl pushed me back but I kept running.

I rounded the corner and that's when I saw Justin holding a boy up against a locker, by the neck. Harrison was flapping and walking in circles. A crowd had gathered.

"Justin!" I screamed. "Stop!" I ran over to him and pulled at the back of his shirt.

"This kid is a bully," hissed Justin.

"I know — but *don't*." I yanked him off of the boy. "Let him go."

Justin drooped like a deflated tire. He backed away from the boy but kept his eye on him. "Give me his backpack," he snarled.

With trembling hands, the kid threw it to Justin. Justin snatched it. "You're a piece of shit."

I glanced up and down the hall. The crowd had dissipated with the next class starting in seconds. So far no teachers had shown up. As much as I wanted to go to the office and tell someone about the bullying, I knew Justin would take the brunt of it because he was the one who had a kid up against a locker. He's already been kicked out of one school for fighting, so he would be the one to get in trouble. That's just the way it worked. I glared at the other boys and said, "Walk away. Or I'll go to the office and say you were bullying Harrison."

"He started the fight," the first boy said, pointing to Justin.

"Seriously?" I barked. "*You* started the bullying. He's right you know — you're all pieces of shit. I'll put this all over social media."

Grumbling, the guys walked away.

"I hate kids like them," said Justin with venom in his voice.

He turned and walked over to Harrison who was still

walking in circles. After last night, I was worried about Harrison, and I didn't want to approach him in case he freaked out on me again. I watched as Justin talked to him. I couldn't hear what he was saying but it seemed to soothe him and he stopped walking and flapping. When Harrison put his backpack on his back, I breathed.

"I'm going to walk him to the office," said Justin. "He wants to see Mrs. Beddington."

"I'll come with you," I said.

We walked on either side of Harrison and he seemed to be okay, although he was having a hard time avoiding the lines between the tiles. I'd never seen him do that before. When we hit Mrs. Beddington's office, she smiled and ushered Harrison into her office. Of course he had to do his door ritual. Justin explained a little about what happened and she kept nodding.

"Okay, I can deal with him now," she said. "Do you know the names of the boys?"

Justin looked away.

"Kyle," said Harrison. "He went to my elementary school and once he put my head in the urinal."

Mrs. Beddington wrote the name on a piece of paper. "That's good, Harrison. Do you have a last name?"

By the time we left Mrs. Beddington's office, Harrison had given the names of the boys, and the bell for class had long gone. Justin squeezed his fists together and said, "I could have punched that kid's lights out."

"What good would that have done?" I asked. "You know you would have been the one suspended."

"More like *they* would have been suspended and I would

have been *kicked out*. When they let me into this school I was told if I fought, even once, I was gone."

"It wouldn't have accomplished anything," I said.

"I can't go back to class."

I eyed him and saw something raw in his eyes. "Let's go outside," I said. "Get some fresh air."

"*You're* going to skip?"

"First time for everything," I said.

We went outside and found a bench facing the sun. It was another gorgeous autumn day although the air was cooler. Sometimes it snowed on Halloween. Justin slouched forward and held his head in his hands. I put my hand on his back and rubbed it.

"You want to talk?" I asked.

For a few moments there was silence between us. Then in a low voice he said, "My sister was bullied at school. It was awful." He shook his head. "I can't stand kids who treat others like crap, especially when all they are is different. It's not right. And they always get away with it."

"I'm sorry about your sister." I kept rubbing, gently. "That must be so hard to have to live with."

"Faith is dead you know." His voice was flat.

My heart almost froze in my chest. My hand stopped rubbing his back. Dead? No wonder he was a mess and avoided talking about her. The guy was always trying to hold in his emotions until he burst in a fit of anger.

"Oh, Justin," I said. "I'm so sorry. I had no idea."

He sat up, exhaled, and leaned back, looking upwards to the white clouds drifting across the blue sky. I waited for him to talk.

"She was bullied," he finally said shaking his head. "It's what killed her. They teased her so much she stopped eating or if she did eat, because we made her, she just went to the bathroom and puked it all up. We tried to help her but nothing worked. My parents even put her in this rehab place for girls with eating disorders. Of course, when she died, the doctors said it was malnutrition that killed her but I don't agree. It was the bullying."

"That must have been so hard for your entire family," I said.

"My parents are still a mess. They blame themselves. And I don't help matters."

"Is that…why you got in a fight at your old school?"

He nodded. "I beat the kid up who hurt her the most. His parents pressed charges and they won."

He lifted his head, narrowed his eyes, and clenched his fists. "Those kids always win and they are just mean assholes with no spines. They hurt kids who can't defend themselves. They drove her crazy, teased her, and tormented her. But in the end, she didn't have any bruises and the guy who I beat up, the one who mentally killed her, did. So I was the bad guy."

"How old was Faith when…?"

"Thirteen. She would have been fourteen in November." Once again he put his head in his hands. "Our house is like a morgue. My mom still hasn't done a thing with her room. I have to walk by it every day."

"That's understandable," I said.

"She loved horses. Going to the barn was such a thrill. I took her three times a week." He smiled but it was a sad smile and tears welled in his eyes. "She loved cooking shows too. She could recite recipes like Harrison recites bones. And she always lined her toy horses up on her shelves." He laughed a sad laugh. "If I moved one even a tiny bit she knew."

"What else did she love?" I asked.

"Me," he said. He paused and wiped his eyes. "She loved me. We used to sit on the sofa and she'd rest her head on my shoulder and hold my hand. When she was upset, she rocked. I knew something was going downhill with her because she started rocking more and more. But I wasn't in her school then. I was in high school." His shoulders started to shake. "I just couldn't, I couldn't protect her anymore."

My heart felt heavy for him. I wanted to cry too. "It's not your fault," I said. I put my hand on his arm.

He continued. "At home we couldn't get her to eat. My mother tried so hard. I did too. She loved ice cream and I would take her to her favourite place but she wouldn't have any. The kids at school knew she was obsessed with cooking shows so they stole her lunch every damn day."

"Why are kids so mean?" I asked. "It makes no sense to me."

"I dunno. Makes them feel good about themselves, I guess. They think they're better than the person they're hurting." He made a funny noise with his lips, blowing out air, and shook his head. "I don't think I can talk about this anymore." He exhaled and sat up straight.

"That's okay," I said, softly.

He turned and looked me in the eyes. "This is the most I've said since her memorial last spring. Not one kid from her school came. She had no friends."

A tear on his cheek glistened in the sun and I reached out

and wiped it away, leaving my finger to rest on his skin.

"Thanks," he said, taking my hand and kissing my knuckles. "For listening."

Under the fall sun, he pulled me close to him. We stayed entangled for a few moments until he put his hand on my face and drew me into him, pressing his lips against mine. Shocked, my response was to inhale his breath, his smell, his touch, and kiss him back. Electricity flowed through me, zapping every one of my nerves, igniting a deep-rooted energy inside me. Without hesitation I allowed myself to kiss him back like I'd never done before.

At the end of the school day, I waited for Justin to give him a ride home and I also waited for Joel and Harrison. Just after lunch, I'd got a text from Joel asking me what happened. When I explained, he wanted to meet up after school. I was leaning against the wall, firing off a text to Marnie when a voice in the distance said, "We missed you in class, Anna." Immediately I looked up to see Mr. Ullrich, my physics teacher, strolling by.

"Um," I said. "I had an appointment."

He nodded and kept walking. *Ouch.* The school always phoned home about absences that weren't recorded. I had to get home before my mother did. Marnie texted back but I didn't tell her I was meeting up with Joel because I didn't want her coming around and flirting. Today, because of the circumstance surrounding the meeting, that would be plain wrong.

Within minutes of seeing Mr. Ullrich, I saw Joel, but Harrison wasn't with him.

"Hey," he said, running his hands through his hair and looking like he was in a huge hurry. "What happened today?"

"Some kids stole Harrison's backpack. My friend Justin, the Chapter President for the Best Buddies program, intervened."

Joel nodded. "Who were they?"

I shrugged. "I'm not entirely sure but I'm pretty sure one was Kyle Fischer."

Joel shook his head in disgust. "He went to Harrison's elementary and junior high school and has done stuff to him for years. I heard a fight almost broke out."

"Yeah. It got stopped before anything major happened, though."

"That's good," he said. "Kyle's father is a lawyer. Once my mother went to the school about him teasing Harrison and Kyle's father managed to make his kid look like a prince. I wanted to beat the living crap out of him. My parents told me I wouldn't win doing something like that and they didn't want me in juvie."

"How's Harrison?" I asked.

"My mom picked him up. I have practice tonight. He's okay. He'll live. I just wanted to know what happened." He had already started to back away from me. "Thanks," he said.

"No problem."

I watched him walk away then break out into a run. *He'll live.* Is that what Justin thought about his sister?

# CHAPTER THIRTEEN
## HARRISON

My mother and brother were raising their voices at each other in the kitchen. I could hear them from the hallway. I wanted to go into the kitchen and set the table because it was 5:45. I set the table every day at 5:45.

"Where were you today when Harrison was getting bullied?" My mother asked this to Joel who had just come home from his hockey practice.

"I told you, I was studying in the library," said Joel.

"You are not telling the truth, Joel. You didn't go to school today because I got a message on my machine saying you were absent."

"I did so go to school," Joel raised his voice again. "Anyway, I thought you put Harrison in that program to let me have some air."

Why would Joel need air? Joel could get enough air by breathing in oxygen and exhaling carbon dioxide. I thought I'd better tell my mother and Joel this so they would stop yelling at each other. Yelling bothered me. It surprised me that they didn't know something so simple.

"Air does not mean skipping class and going to Amy's.

That girl is not good for you." My mother said this to Joel as I walked into the kitchen.

"Joel can get air from breathing oxygen," I said.

"What are you talking about?" Joel asked me.

"If you need air you should just breathe in oxygen and exhale carbon dioxide."

"I give up," said Joel. He left the kitchen, stomping his feet and when he got to his room, he slammed the door. The noise could be heard in the kitchen. Even I knew that slamming the door meant he was angry about something.

I went to the cupboard and got the dishes out to put them on the table because that is what I do every day. As I was placing the plates on the placemats, my mother asked me, "Harrison, did you thank Anna today?"

"I thanked her last night," I said. My mother had heard me thank her for coming to dinner.

"I meant for helping you today at school."

"Would that have been appropriate?" I asked.

"Yes, under the circumstances. Was it Kyle who took your backpack?"

"Yes," I said. "I don't like him."

"I don't blame you," she said. "From now on when someone does that to you, just walk away and go to the office."

"I had a ham sandwich today for lunch. I wanted my ham sandwich."

"Would you like to be homeschooled?" my mother asked.

I put down the last plate. "No," I said. "If I was home-schooled, I couldn't be in the Best Buddies program and go to the dance with my girlfriend, Anna, and wear my new shirt from the Science Centre."

"Harrison," said my mother. Just by the way she said my name I knew she had her eyebrows squished together. I looked at her and I was right.

"Yes," I answered her.

"Anna is your *friend*. She is not your *girlfriend*."

"If she is my friend and she is a girl then she is my girlfriend."

"Okay. Just don't read anything more into the situation."

"She's not a book, Mom. I can't *read* into the situation."

"You're right. That was a bad choice of words on my part. I guess what I'm saying is she is your friend and she is a girl but she is not your girlfriend. You aren't going to do the things that boys and girls do when they are boyfriend and girlfriend, like hold hands and kiss."

I opened the cutlery drawer and picked out four forks, four knives, and four spoons. Why did everyone think I was going to kiss Anna?

"Kissing can cause —"

"Don't start, okay? We're about to eat."

Dinner was ready and Joel was still up in his room. "I'll be right back," said my mother, wiping her hands on a dishcloth before leaving the kitchen. My dad had just got home and he had changed and was in his at-home clothes and was mashing the potatoes. My dad had work clothes and at-home clothes. My mother was gone exactly three minutes and two seconds and when she walked into the kitchen, Joel was with her.

"Hey," said my dad to Joel. "How goes the battle?"

I wasn't sure who Joel was battling but I did know he had a hockey game on the weekend and sometimes he pushed his opponents around.

"Not great. Mom is ragging on me again."

"I'm not ragging on him. I just have some questions."

Dad put the potatoes on the table. I could eat mashed potatoes and roast beef and corn because everything could be separate on my plate.

"Why don't we just sit down and enjoy dinner," Mom said.

Today I ate what my family ate, except the gravy. I didn't like gravy on my potatoes. I was putting some roast beef on my plate when my dad spoke. "Joel, you ready for your home opener on the weekend?"

"Yeah," Joel mumbled. I glanced at his plate and saw that everything except his vegetables was covered with gravy.

"Should be a good game," said my dad.

Sometimes I went to Joel's games and if a lot of people were in the stands my parents would let me play with my video game and wear a headset so I wouldn't have to hear the crowd cheering. Playoff games or final tournament games are the ones where I've got to block out the noise. I bent my head and focused on what was on my plate. My parents and Joel talked in the distance.

When I was finished, I looked up.

"Are you done?" my mother asked me.

"Yes," I said.

"Are you coming to my game this weekend, Harrison?" Joel asked me.

I looked at my mother. "Am I going to Joel's game?"

"Sure," said my mom.

"I think your Best Buddy's friend might be coming," said Joel.

"Maybe you should ask Anna to come," said my mother. "Instead of going to the Science Centre again."

"She'd probably like that," muttered Joel.

"Joel," said my mother as if he'd said something wrong, which he hadn't. It was true. Maybe she would like to go to the game.

After dinner, I said to my mother, "I'm going to phone Anna and thank her for helping me today and ask her to come to Joel's game with me."

"I think that is a good idea," she said. "*Friends* can do things like that."

Since the phone I liked to use was in the family room I went in there. My dad sat in his favourite chair, a recliner, and he was reading the newspaper.

"I heard you had a little incident at school," he said. "I'm sorry to hear that."

"It's okay," I said. "Next time I'm going to go to the office even if I have a ham sandwich."

"Smart boy."

He went back to reading his newspaper and I picked up the phone. One ring. Two rings. Three rings. Four rings. I was about to hang up because I couldn't be on the phone if it rang five times but Anna answered.

"Hello, Anna," I said after she said hello to me. "This is Harrison Henry."

"Hi, Harrison." Her voice sounded higher than usual and a little louder. Why was she talking like this? She sounded excited that I had called, kind of like Joel's girlfriends when he was playing around with them and lifting them off the ground. That's when they always laughed in a high-pitched voice. I didn't like how she sounded.

"I wanted to say thank you for helping me today."

"Oh, it was no problem, Harrison. I'm just glad I got there before those boys did anything else. How are you doing now?"

"I'm fine," I said. "Next time someone takes my backpack in the hall I'm going to go to the office even if I have a ham sandwich."

"That's a great idea."

"Mrs. Beddington told me to do that and so did my parents. I like Mrs. Beddington."

"Yeah, me too. She's awesome."

"My mother thinks that I should ask you to my brother Joel's hockey game."

"What another great idea, Harrison," said Anna. "I would love that!" She sounded very happy on the phone because her voice was elevated and had a ring to it. It made me happy to think that I knew that she was happy. Sometimes I didn't know when people were happy.

"Since you had an idea of where we could go, I also have an idea," she said. "I was wondering if you would like to go to the grocery store with me to pick up some food for the Halloween dance. Then we could pick out the kind of food you like to eat."

"I've been to the grocery store with my mother. I think I could do that."

"Okay. What day would be good for you?"

"I will ask my mother."

I put the phone down and went to find her.

"I can drive you tomorrow after school," said my mother when I asked her about driving me to the grocery store.

"I have to watch *Grey's Anatomy*."

She nodded. "After that then. I will take you. But ask her if it works for her. That's important."

I went back to the phone and picked it up. "My mother said she would drive me to the grocery store tomorrow after *Grey's Anatomy*. She also told me to ask if that works for you."

"Yes, that works. Now I should ask you, do you know what time the hockey game begins?"

"The puck will drop at exactly 7:00 pm at the Memorial Arena, which is located on 127 Church Street."

"Great," she said. "I can meet *you* there. Just like you're meeting me at the grocery store. I'm excited about the game, Harrison."

I hung up the phone and my father said, "Well done, kid."

"Thank you, Dad."

I went to my room to do my homework and when I was about halfway through my math, my mother came up to my door and knocked. I hoped she didn't want to talk about my English because I wasn't going to do it until we had to read another story. I did not want to read about the monkey's paw.

"Yes," I said.

"Alan is here. Are you okay to have him visit for an hour or so?"

"Yes," I said.

"Have you done your English?"

"No and I'm not doing it. Tell Alan he can come in my room."

Alan arrived at my door in fifty-six seconds and he walked in wearing his backpack. He shut my door. "I have my computer in my backpack," he whispered.

"I'm not allowed a computer in my room," I said. Alan knew that, so why did he bring his computer over? My parents had put a ban on me having a computer in my room because then I didn't do my homework. I also was on a cell phone ban because I played too many games. I looked at Alan's backpack. "Your backpack has germs," I said.

Alan pulled his computer out of his bag and put his backpack outside my door.

"The computer is mine, not yours," said Alan, "and I'm taking it home with me so it's not like *you* have a computer in your room. Well, you do but only for a short time."

"Why did you bring it?" I asked.

"I thought we could search for more ideas on how to build better Lego robots. They do that in the Lego Mind Storm Club. There are so many videos online. And I was also thinking that we could do a video. Our robot is better than the ones they're building in the school club. There's a girl in the club and she really likes watching the videos and she's not very tall and she's pretty. Maybe if she saw me in one she would like me back."

Alan plunked his computer on my desk and turned it on.

"Don't sit in my chair," I said.

"Oh right," he said. He was short so he could just look over my shoulder and we would be almost the same height.

I sat down and wiped off his computer with an anti-bacterial wipe. Alan stood beside me, waiting. After the computer was clean, I said, "I'm going to a hockey game with Anna."

"Is that like a date?" His breath felt warm on my neck.

"I don't like you breathing on me," I said. Alan moved a step to my side. Now I could answer his question. "She's a girl and she's my friend but she's not my girlfriend," I said.

"If you kiss her, she can be your girlfriend."

"I don't want to," I said.

"You might have to," he said. "Before we look up Mind Storm videos, I've got an idea." Alan pulled the computer over to him and typed in 'boys and girls kissing instructions.'

"Why are we looking this up?" I asked.

"There are so many videos on how to do it," said Alan. "Like millions. Like tons."

"A ton is weight," I said, "not a number."

"Well, then there are millions. Seriously, man. You have to learn how to do this," he said. "Look, here's a video on how to have your first kiss. Let's watch it."

I exited out of the video to get back to the Google home page. "No. I told you kissing is an exchange of germs. Let's look up Lego Robot videos."

"Fine," he sighed. "But dude, you've got some serious issues when it comes to girls."

# CHAPTER FOURTEEN
## ANNA

O h crap. My mother's car was in the driveway. My palms
started to sweat. My heart picked up its pace. What if
the school had phoned about me skipping? Maybe if I went
in the back door I could sneak to my room. If she was in her
office and not in the kitchen I would be okay.

As soon as I had squeaked open the back door, I heard
her voice, "Anna, is that you?"

Busted.

"Yup," I said. Now, I had no choice but see her because
I had to walk through the kitchen to get to my room. She was
probably drinking coffee.

"How was school?" she asked when I slouched into the
kitchen.

"Fine." I went to the cupboard, got a glass, and filled it
with water as I tried to steal glances at the answering machine to
see if the light was beeping. We had cell phones so the landline
wasn't used a ton and it was an old-fashioned one. No red light.

"I should go to my room though and get my homework
done." I tried to walk by her but she grabbed my arm.

"Honey, we need to talk."

I lowered my head and stared at the tiles on the floor, waiting for the lecture about skipping school and missing a college fair and how all this combined would hurt my chances for university. I cringed when I thought about the 85% on my English essay.

"Why do you think I have given up on you?" she asked.

Well, that was unexpected.

"Or gave up on you when you were just a baby?" Her voice sounded hurt and sad.

I sucked in a deep breath and lifted my chin to look at her. *Speak*, I thought. *Now's your chance.*

"All you care about are my grades," I said.

"That's not true." She touched my cheek.

"It seems to me that if I do well in school, I'm a good kid. That's when you're most proud of me. That's when you are *interested* in me. You want me to be like you. A workaholic."

"I love my job. Is that wrong?"

"No." She always nailed me and I never won arguments with her. She had been to law school and had practised criminal law until she became a judge. She won a lot of battles in the courtroom by badgering people. Although, I had to admit, she wasn't badgering me now. She was using her soft-voice tactic.

"You've always striven to do well in school, so I've wanted that for you too."

"I don't want to go to Princeton, Mom. I want to try something different."

She tucked a strand of my hair behind my ear and it reminded me of when I was little. She used to do that to me all the time and I liked it, and I still did. "Okay. Let's think about this. Apply to them all and in the spring, you can pick your school." She paused for a moment before she eyed me. "But, skipping school isn't going to help you get in anywhere."

"I know." I hung my head again. She was right on that one.

"Why didn't you go to class?"

"Something happened with Harrison. I had to help."

"Oh, Anna." She sighed and I heard the disappointment. I'd been hearing it since I was little. "This program is not helping you at all. Seriously, the teachers should be dealing with these problems. Why didn't you talk to a teacher, so you could get to class?"

"You don't understand what I'm doing — what I'm trying to do," I said just as my chicken-dance ringtone sounded. I pulled my phone out of my pocket and when I saw it was Harrison I moved away from her. "Speaking of Harrison." I answered after the fourth ring so I could see her closing her eyes in irritation.

"Hi, Harrison," I said loudly, just to bug her some more. I also tried to add a cheery inflection in my voice.

Of course he told me who he was, like he did every time we talked. I smiled.

"I wanted to say thank you for helping me today," he said.

"Oh, it was no problem, Harrison." I made sure I looked at my mother when I said this. "I'm just glad I got there before those boys did anything else. How are you doing now?"

"I'm fine," he said. "Next time someone takes my backpack in the hall I'm going to go to the office even if I have a ham sandwich."

"That's a great idea." I emphasized the word *great*.

"Mrs. Beddington told me to do that and so did my parents. I like Mrs. Beddington."

"Yeah, me too." Again, I used my chipper, cheerful voice. "She's awesome."

"For our Best Buddy time this week," he said, "my mother thinks that I should ask you to my brother Joel's hockey game."

"What another great idea, Harrison." I glanced at my mother. She was trying so hard not to scowl but it wasn't working. "I would love that!" This time I almost gushed, which I knew was wrong but I did it anyways. Then I had an idea.

"I was also wondering if you would like to go to the grocery store with me to pick up some food for the Halloween dance. Then you could pick out the food you like to eat."

"I've been to the grocery store with my mother," he said with confidence. "I think I could do that."

"Okay. What day would be good for you?"

"I will ask my mother."

I heard him put the phone down and I waited, sneaking glances at my mother who was muttering as she opened the oven door. Was she actually cooking something? Within a minute, Harrison returned and said, "My mother said she would drive me to the grocery store tomorrow after *Grey's Anatomy*. She also told me to ask if that works for you."

"Yes, that works. Now I should ask you, do you know what time the hockey game begins?"

He gave me the details about the time and place, then I said, "Great! I can meet *you* there. Just like you're meeting me at the grocery store. I'm excited about the game, Harrison."

When I hung up, my mother's lips were pursed. I whistled as I opened the fridge and took out an apple. "What's for dinner tonight?"

"Do *you like* this boy?" She asked from across the room

and I could feel her eyes boring holes into me. As a judge, she had eyes that could penetrate the thickest skin.

I turned and looked at her. "Of course I *like* him. I'm his Best Buddy and I'm helping him. That's my role in the program. And he's a sweet kid."

"You're not helping him by flirting with him. You know that, right?"

"I wasn't flirting." I frowned at her. "That would be *unethical.*"

"Well, it sounded to me like you were flirting with him on the phone."

"Well, FYI, I wasn't."

The look she gave me made me want to sink into the floor. I'd seen it before, in the courthouse, when she was talking to someone who had done something wrong. It was her I-know-what-you've-done-and-I-don't-buy-your-lie look.

I turned my head so I wouldn't have to see her eyes. "Should I order the pizza?" I snapped.

"No," she said. "I'm making chicken tonight. I thought we could have a family meal."

After dinner (which was just okay because my mom burned the rice and her chicken was bland) I went to my room. First thing I did was text Justin. He called me within seconds.

"Hey," I said, sitting cross-legged on my bed. My room had a canopy bed but my bedding had never been pink. Always neutral tones. My mother hadn't wanted me to be a girly girl. Said they didn't go anywhere in life. My favourite movie as a twelve-year-old was *Legally Blonde* and I watched it over and over to bug my mother. Finally, she'd banned it.

"Did your parents find out about today?" I asked.

"Just about me skipping class — not about my *almost* fight. Got the automated phone call and I didn't get home in time to erase it."

"Yeah, me too," I said.

"I'm sorry about that. You didn't have to get in trouble for me."

"It's okay. No biggie. I got the homework." I paused for a moment before I said, "I think I'm going to Harrison's brother's game this weekend."

"Should be a good game," he said. "I've played against Joel. He's their best player by far."

"You played hockey?"

"Yeah."

"When?"

"Since I was five."

"Do you still play?" He had never mentioned playing hockey to me, ever.

"No," he said. "I had to quit."

"Oh," I said. I paused for just a moment before I asked, "Because of Faith?"

"My fight didn't go over well with my school, and since I was on a school team when I got kicked out, well, no more hockey."

"You could have tried out for our team. This year."

"I didn't want to."

"Do you miss it?"

"Yeah. All the time."

"Why don't you come with me on Saturday night?" I asked. "I'm meeting Harrison there."

"I'll think about it," he said.

The next day I waited outside the grocery store for Harrison. When his mother drove up, she got out of the car and motioned for me to come over.

"How long do you think you'll be?" she asked.

"Twenty minutes tops," I said.

She nodded. "Great. I'll do some banking."

Harrison and I walked into the grocery store and I was pleased to see that it wasn't too busy. "Should we go to the produce section?" I asked.

"The only vegetables I like are green beans and corn. But I like bananas."

"I think corn might be hard to put on a veggie tray," I laughed. "Kind of hard to dip. But we could probably get bananas and cut them into chunks."

"I don't like sharing dips," he said, not joining in my laughter.

We walked over to the plastic cartons of berries. "What about strawberries?" I asked.

He shook his head. "They have a lot of seeds."

"What about cut carrots?"

"I only like green beans and corn."

"Okay," I said. This was going to be harder than I thought. "What food would you like to see at the dance?"

"I don't like anything touching. And I don't like dipping

food. I don't eat nachos. And I don't want to eat chips after someone has put their hand in the bowl. What if they didn't use sanitizer? I like hot dogs."

"Hot dogs would be hard to do, Harrison. We don't have a kitchen. The dance is in a classroom. Maybe we could do little separate bowls full of chips," I said. "Then you could have your own bowl. Would that work?"

"That would be better," he said.

"Let's get the bananas, then find the aisle with disposable bowls."

Once I had the bananas in my basket, we left the produce section. I was so busy trying to read the aisle signs that I bumped into Harrison. He, in turn, bumped into a display of cans. Some went toppling to the tiled floor, making a crashing noise.

"Whoops!" I said. I started to pick up the cans but Harrison just stood ramrod still, frozen in one spot. Then I saw his hands start to flap.

Oh no. Not here. Should I try talking to him? What if he had a meltdown in the grocery store under my watch?

I remembered his breathing techniques so I walked over to him. "Harrison," I said. "It's okay. It wasn't your fault. Just breathe, okay?"

He did as I told him and his hands stopped flapping.

Then out of the blue, I heard an all-too-familiar voice. "Anna?"

My mother.

A look of panic crossed Harrison's face. His hands flapped again.

"Not now, Mom," I said, without even looking at her. "Harrison, keep breathing, okay?"

His hands were still flapping but he kept breathing.

"Is it okay if I pick up the cans, Harrison?" I asked.

He nodded.

Only three had fallen so I picked them up and put them back on the display. "See?" I said. "It's okay."

He nodded. His flapping stopped. "Once I saw a woman step on a can in a grocery store and she fell and I made my mother wait until a paramedic came and he said he thought the woman's arm was broken. I knew it was the ulna or the radius that was broken. I told the paramedic which bones were broken even though my mother told me to keep quiet. She tried to make me go home before they came but I refused. The bones of the lower arm are the ulna and radius and the bone in the upper arm is the humerus."

"That's really good that you stayed to help her. Would you like to leave now?"

He nodded.

"Do you need help?" my mother asked.

Harrison froze and his hands started flapping again.

"No. I don't." I had to keep my focus on Harrison. Keep him calm. "Come on, Harrison," I said. "Walk with me. We'll go outside and wait for your mother."

Harrison walked beside me, and we left my mother standing in the aisle. Was she staring at me? I had no idea and I didn't care.

As soon as we were outside, (minus the bananas) I could see Harrison's body relax, the tension hissing right out of him as if he was a tire losing air.

"Good job," I said.

"The bones of the lower arm are the ulna and radius and

the bone in the upper arm is the humerus."

I let him recite bones until his mother showed up. As soon as he saw her, he bolted over to the car. When his mother leaned over to open the front door, he got in the back.

I walked over to the car as well and she put the passenger-side window down. "Is everything okay?"

"We had a little collision with some cans. A few fell on the floor," I said.

She nodded. "That's enough explanation for me. Been there, done that."

"He handled it really well," I said.

"Thanks so much," she said. "We really appreciate what you're doing for him."

I smiled. "Will I see you at the game on Friday?"

She smiled back. "Yes, for sure."

From the back seat, I heard Harrison's voice. "Thank you, Anna. I look forward to seeing you on Friday night."

"Me too, Harrison," I said.

On Friday night, I got dressed, making sure I was wearing flat shoes. I'd only ever been to one hockey game before. I'd hardly had any time all week to hang out with Justin so I had offered to drive. We had made a date to go for pizza after. Of course, Marnie was coming to the game too. Somehow she'd already met Joel through her hockey friend at some party that I wasn't invited to. She'd also found out he'd broken up with his on-again-off-again girlfriend, Amy. Marnie moved faster than me, ran in more popular crowds, but I didn't care. Never had. Justin and I were moving at our pace and that suited me just fine.

Justin wasn't out front when I pulled up to his house, so I parked and turned my car off. I stepped out of my car, walked to the front door, and knocked.

A pudgy man with a teddy bear face opened the door. "Hello," he said.

"Is Justin here?"

He ushered me in. "You must be Anna."

Had Justin mentioned me to his parents? I sure hadn't mentioned him to my mom. Once I was inside I stuck out my hand, "Anna Leonard," I said. "Pleased to meet you."

He gave me a small but warm smile. The house was darkly lit, curtains were closed, and a weird sadness oozed from the walls.

"Justin is talking to his mother. He'll be down in a moment."

We stood in the front entrance, making small talk until Justin walked down the stairs. "Anna," he said. There was a brief, awkward pause. "I didn't know you were here."

"We've had a nice chat," said his father. "How's your mother?"

"She's asleep," he said.

His father sighed and said, "Good." Then he patted Justin's back. "Have a good time."

As we drove away from his house, I asked tentatively, "Is your mom sick?"

"She's barely got out of bed since Faith died," he said.

"That's so sad. I can't imagine how hard it is for her."

"Yeah," he said. "It's been hard on all of us." He stared out the window. "But there are days when I wish she would just get it together. I'm her kid too but it's almost as if I don't count."

"I'm sure that's not how it is," I said.

He slouched in his seat. "I don't want to talk about her."

We didn't talk about anything more on the drive to the rink, and I wasn't going to ask any more questions. But in the parking lot, I was about to get out of the car when he touched my arm. "Thanks," he said.

"For what?"

"I'm glad I'm going to this game. It makes me feel like I'm living." He pulled me close and nuzzled his nose into my hair. His warm breath on my skin made my heart race. I wanted to taste his lips. Over the years I'd had a few guys kiss me, but none had ever made me feel the way Justin did. I moved my head to encourage him and when our lips touched, I almost groaned out loud.

After we'd broken apart, I could hardly breathe. I rested my cheek on his and we stayed in that position for a few seconds. Then he whispered, "We'd better go in."

"Yeah," I said. "Harrison will be waiting."

As we walked into the arena he took my hand in his. Upon entering the lobby, I saw Marnie first and she waved in huge gestures, of course. She raced over to us, her long, red hair flowing behind her, the smile on her face enormous. "Rah, rah," she said.

"Yeah, rah, rah," I said. "Marnie, this is Justin. Justin, Marnie."

Justin raised his hand and gave her a cool two-finger wave.

"It's great to meet you. I've heard a lot about you." Marnie flashed her biggest smile.

I rolled my eyes at her. Then I glanced around the lobby.

"Have you seen Harrison?" I asked. "I'm supposed to meet him here."

"I think he's hiding behind the vending machine," she said.

I scanned the lobby and sure enough there he was, standing beside the vending machine, looking like he was hiding from the crowd. I let go of Justin's hand and waved. Harrison didn't wave back but that was okay; sometimes he just couldn't because of the stimulation.

We walked over to him. "Hi, Harrison," I said.

"What is he doing here?" he asked, and quite bluntly too. "I'm supposed to be meeting you. Not him."

# CHAPTER FIFTEEN
## HARRISON

The fabric on the new pants my mother had bought for me felt scratchy so I changed. I heard my mother's voice on the other side of my door. "Harrison," she said, "it's time to go."

Yes, I knew that. Every second that went by, I sweated a little more under my armpits. I didn't like the feeling because I had put on deodorant and it was supposed to help but today it wasn't and perhaps I was sweating because I was still changing. How could I be late? I didn't want to be late. My hands started to flap. I had to stop them. I wanted to go to the game and meet Anna.

The tan pants felt better. I tucked my shirt in and opened my door.

"Are you okay?" my mother asked.

"Yes," I said.

"All right. Your father is waiting in the car. He wants to see Joel's team warm up." She patted my back. "You look nice, Harrison."

"So do you."

"Why, thank you."

"I saw someone say that on television," I said.

She gave me the thumbs up. "Let's go, handsome."

The arena wasn't far away and we got there early. In the lobby, I glanced at my watch. Anna would arrive in thirteen minutes if she wasn't late or early. My parents went to sit down but I told my mother I wanted to wait in the lobby for Anna and to save us two seats, preferably at the end of the row so I didn't have to walk by knees to get to my seat. Nine minutes went by and Anna hadn't come through the doors yet. She had told me on the phone that she would meet me at 6:55 because the game started at 7:00.

At 6:50 she walked through the front door with Justin, the boy who ran the Best Buddies program and they were holding hands. She was five minutes early. Why was Justin with her? My mother had saved two seats, not three. She didn't see me and walked right over to a girl named Marnie. Marnie and Joel had talked in the hall at school yesterday and I'd had to wait and I got home at 3:28 and almost missed watching *Grey's Anatomy*. Joel didn't kiss Marnie but he touched her face and she smiled at him and looked in his eyes. I told my mother that Joel had a new girlfriend and they had touched in the hallway and he had yelled at me and my mother had told him to stop. I told him to breathe. Then he told me to shut up.

Marnie was laughing again. And so was Anna. Justin was still holding her hand. I thought about holding her hand. Maybe I could do that if I had a lot of hand sanitizer. But I couldn't hold her hand today, not after she had held hands with Justin because he would have germs and I would get his germs and I had only brought one small bottle of hand sanitizer. Why did she come with him? My mother had only saved two seats, not three. I would have to tell her to use hand sanitizer too. I wanted my hands to stop flapping so I lowered my head and stared at the floor and they stopped.

"Harrison." I heard Anna's voice. I lifted my head but I didn't look her in the eyes. Justin stood beside her.

"Why is he here?" I asked. My mother had only saved two seats. "I'm supposed to be meeting you, not him."

Anna squeezed her hands together. "Um, he likes hockey and wants to watch your brother," she said.

"My mother only saved two seats." My hands started to flap. It was impossible for three of us to sit in two seats. The seats weren't big enough to share.

"That's okay," said Justin. "I can stand along the boards or sit with Marnie. Why don't you two go in and sit down? The game is going to start."

"Yes," I said. "We need to go to our seats." We had to get to our seats. I hoped my parents had arrived early enough to secure the seats close to the edge. I didn't like having to pass by people's knees. I quickly glanced at my watch. "The game begins in two minutes."

"Let's meet in between periods," said Justin.

Anna and I walked into the part of the arena where the ice was and there were so many people I could hardly get through the door and when I tried to stick my foot over the line first to test it someone pushed me from behind. My hands started to flap so I stuck them in my pockets and walked forward, and now that I was over the line I tried not to touch shoulders with anyone. There were too many people, too many shoulders, and too much noise. Quickly, I looked around for my parents. The crowd was big and noisy and the sounds of everyone talking were inside my head. I couldn't let the words get trapped. I didn't have room to walk in circles because there were too many people and I would bump into them. I tried to breathe. Then I saw my parents. They were sitting on the edge and I could see the two seats they were saving and this allowed me to breathe. I put my head down and walked right over to the stands and up the stairs and sat down.

"Where's Anna?" my mother asked.

I glanced up and when I didn't see her, my hands started to flap. We were supposed to sit together. My mother had saved two seats.

"Did you wait for her?" my mother asked.

"No. I had to get through the door and by a lot of people."

"You should be aware of the other person when you are both going to the same place together. Do you understand that, Harrison?"

"No," I said. "I told her we had saved her a seat. I didn't like the crowd."

"There she is," said my mother.

Anna was below us, scanning the crowd.

"Anna!" My mother called out to her and waved.

Anna waved back and climbed the stairs leading to the seat my mother had saved.

"I lost you," she said when she was sitting down. "Sorry about that."

Just then the buzzer sounded and the game started. "Joel is on right wing. His number is 19 and he is on the team with the red-and-navy jerseys. He's always worn the number 19 because it is his favourite number. My favourite number is 8."

My mother cheered loudly when Joel scored with three minutes and twenty-three seconds left in the first period. Anna cheered too. I put my hands over my ears and I didn't cheer.

The buzzer sounded to end the period. "Would you like to go to the lobby?" Anna asked. "Maybe we could get some popcorn."

I never leave my seat between the first and second periods when I am at a hockey game because the lobby always gets crowded and the line-up for the concessions is too long. And people drink coffee and I don't like coffee.

"No," I said. "I'll stay here."

"Could I bring you some popcorn?" she asked. "Or a drink?"

"I don't like popcorn and a drink will make me have to go to the restroom and I still don't like public restrooms."

My mother leaned over again. "Anna, that's nice of you to ask," she said.

Anna nodded and then she stood. "I'll be right back," she said.

As soon as she'd gone, my mother said, "You should have said 'no, thank you,' and perhaps not mentioned about how you don't like to use the restrooms, which, by the way, is something we still need to work on."

"I *don't* like them," I said.

"Remember that you don't always have to say everything that is on your mind. Now if you'll excuse me I'm going to go to the restroom and you can sit with your father." She handed me my Nintendo DS.

Why was it okay for her to say she had to go to the restroom but not okay for me to say that I didn't like them? And my therapist always told me to talk to get things out of my head so there was less to process, and here was my mother telling me to keep the words in my head.

My dad didn't talk to me and that was fine with me because I wanted to play my video game anyway. I got to the fourth accident, one about a boy on a bike getting run over by a car and the boy broke his femur, which is the thigh bone and the largest bone in the body, when my mother and Anna came back to the seats. Anna had a bucket of popcorn and a drink.

"What game are you playing?" she asked when she sat down.

"*First Responders*," I answered.

"Cool. I've heard of that one."

Most people didn't know anything about the game. "Joel thinks it is a dumb game."

"I've never actually played it," replied Anna, "but I've heard good things about it."

"My favourite game is the one I just played when a boy gets in an accident and breaks his femur. The femur is the largest bone in the body and has a long shaft that looks like a cylinder. It connects medially to the knee joint and —"

"Harrison," said my mother. "Let's talk about something else."

"Would you like some popcorn?" Anna asked, moving the container closer to me.

"No, thank you," I said, remembering what my mother had told me about how to respond to a question when I didn't want something. Then I said, "I don't share food."

"Oh, right. I'm sorry. I forgot," said Anna. "I could have got you a hot dog."

"I like hot dogs," I said.

"I remember that."

At the end of the second period, Joel had two goals. After the buzzer went and all the players had left the ice, my mother said, "Harrison, Anna was talking to some kids from your school in the lobby. Why don't you go with her and meet them? You could get a hot dog."

Why was my mother telling me to do something I didn't want to do? Today, I wanted to sit and play video games in between the second and third period. Usually, my mother asked me what I wanted to do and sometimes I wanted a hot dog and other times I wanted to sit and play my video game and today she was *telling* me to go talk to strangers. Well, except Justin. He wasn't a stranger. I wondered if he was my friend now. Maybe I had three friends: Alan and Justin and Anna. I had gone from having one friend at the beginning of the year to having three friends so that meant I had tripled my friends. Perhaps, today, I could try to do something different and go to the arena lobby and meet my friends, now that I had three. Today I would only meet two of them though because Alan wasn't at the hockey game. My breath started to pick up speed inside my body. I wished I didn't have to always try new things. I liked doing the same thing because it made more sense.

"Go ahead, Harrison," urged my mother. "It will be okay. You follow Anna and I will follow you. If you get uncomfortable we can come back here and you can play your video game."

I stood up. Anna went down the stairs and I followed her. The crowd grew and grew as I walked. I stuck my hands in my pockets and stared at her jacket so I wouldn't get lost. My mother walked behind me and I liked that she was there.

"Keep breathing," she said.

Anna opened the door and held it for me and I walked to

the line, put my foot over it, and pulled it back. I did that three times and a man bumped into me and a woman.

Once I was through the door Anna said, "They are standing over there." She pointed to the vending machine and I saw three people, not two. The girl that Joel had touched but not kissed was there too. I liked where they were standing; that was one of my favourite spots. We went over and I felt good about myself for doing this. Now I might have four friends; two boys that were friends and two girls that were friends. That would mean I had quadrupled my friends.

"Marnie," said Anna. "This is Harrison. Joel's brother."

"Hi, Harrison," said Marnie.

"Hi," I mumbled without lifting my head or looking anyone in the eyes.

"We met yesterday, remember?"

"Yes, I remember," I said. "You were with Joel after school and I got home at 3:27 and by the time I was sitting down in front of the television I only had one minute until *Grey's Anatomy*."

"I like that show too," said Justin. "What's your favourite episode?"

I saw Justin reach for Anna's hand. She wouldn't have washed her hands after eating the popcorn.

"You shouldn't hold hands," I said.

# CHAPTER SIXTEEN
## ANNA

Justin dropped my hand and shoved his in his pocket. "I like the *Time Warp* episode," he said.

"That's my favourite too," said Harrison.

Relief swept through me. We had a new topic.

"I think the information on AIDS in that episode was interesting," said Justin. "What did you think about the episode where the girl has the stomach tumour?"

Harrison prattled on about stomach tumours. Marnie answered her phone and walked away from us. Harrison continued talking until it was time to go back into the arena. Perhaps he had forgotten about Justin and me holding hands.

Again, I took my seat beside him. He handed me some sanitizer and I squirted it on my palm. He seemed unfazed about his holding-hands comment, but I sure wasn't. I thought about it the entire period. Why did he say it? Was my mother right? Was I leading him on? Was he getting jealous?

The game ended and Joel's team won 5-3. Like the hero and the stud that he was, Joel scored three goals.

Mrs. Henry and I walked into the lobby together. "It was nice to see you again," she said.

"Thank you for encouraging Harrison to invite me. I enjoyed the game."

She leaned into me a little and said, "And *thank you* for all you're doing for Harrison. Tonight was a first. Him talking with a group of kids like that." She smiled like *he* was the one who had scored three goals.

"I'm enjoying my time with him," I said.

"Getting that shirt for him to wear to the dance was clever. He is actually excited to go." This time when she smiled she also held one hand to her heart. "I never thought this day would ever come for him."

"I'm sure we'll have fun," I said.

"I'm sure you will too." She put her hand on my arm, in a touchy, motherly gesture. "I had better run. Harrison will be timing me."

As I watched her go, I wished my mother was like her, caring and compassionate and interested in more than just the academics in my life. I jumped when a hand touched my shoulder.

"You ready?" said Justin.

"You snuck up on me." I playfully punched his arm and he grabbed my hand and looked me square in the eyes.

"Nah," he said. "You were just deep in thought." He tilted his head and assessed me. "Are you okay?"

"Yeah, I'm okay. We can talk outside."

Once outside, Justin took my hand in his. I liked the feel of his skin, including the calluses on his palm. After watching the hockey game and seeing the leather gloves they wore, I figured he'd probably toughened his hands when he played. A vision of him braiding a young girl's hair popped into my mind.

He had hands that were good for many things.

He lifted my hand in his and kissed my knuckles. "What were you thinking about in there?"

"My mother. She saw Harrison and me in the grocery store the other day and I managed to get him out of a situation before he had a meltdown and she didn't even mention anything to me. When I got home she was busy working on some huge case."

"What does she do?"

"She's a judge."

"Wow. That's impressive."

I didn't want to talk about my mother's impressive career. "Do you think Harrison is upset with me for holding your hand?" I asked. "Do you think I might be leading him on? Like, our friendship might mean more to him than it should?"

"I don't think so," he said. "But my experience is with my sister. Faith was immature as well and she wouldn't have had a clue about how to be with a boy. So it could be he's just confused and not sure how to even have a friend, let alone a girl who is a friend."

I nodded. "Maybe when we are around him we should just cool the touching."

"It's either that or we continue showing him that we're a couple." He dropped my hand because we were at my car. As he opened the door he said, "It's your call."

"I'll think about it." I got in the car and started the engine.

"Maybe at the dance this Thursday we can introduce him to someone from the Best Buddies program who he can relate to," I said.

"We can try. Don't expect too much from the dance. Just

getting him in the room will be huge. If he stands by the wall, that's fine. The fact that's he's there is what will count."

"Okay," I said.

He reached out and touched my cheek. "He's not with us now."

"Should I find a secluded road?" I asked with a shocking boldness.

"Sounds good to me," he replied, lifting his one eyebrow. "And I know just the one."

The last committee meeting for the dance was on Monday. I had spent most of the weekend with Justin. Our relationship was clipping along at a speed that made me feel as if I was careening down a road in a sports car with the top down. Okay, so, bad cliché. But I seriously could not get enough of him.

I sat across from him while we hashed through the last few details. When Justin put his foot on mine I just wanted to kiss him. It was as if he'd kindled my sense of touch into massive flames. Here I was, Anna the brain, at a school club meeting, playing footsies. The thought almost made me giggle out loud.

"Everything looks good," said Justin. "You guys did a great job." He smiled at Erika and she beamed, her eyes crinkling. I wondered about Justin maybe being paired with someone like her, thinking it would be so good for him.

"I love the idea of the Lego table," said Gianni.

"Harrison helped me with that one," I said. "I can't take the credit."

"I'll tell him thanks."

"So we're all set," said Justin, closing his notebook.

"Let's rock and roll," said Gianni.

"I want to dance," said Erika, giggling and covering her mouth. She stood up and so did Gianni. "We've been practising," she said.

Gianni played with his phone for a minute. When the classical music sounded, they started waltzing. It was so beautiful to watch. I clapped and laughed a deep laugh that came from somewhere in my soul. And I was grateful. This whole experience had become about so much more than just churning out resume padding. I was part of something that was making a real difference.

I wondered if Harrison would dance. Probably not, but that was okay. Justin tapped my shoulder. "Would you like to dance?" he asked, grinning.

I grinned back and let him pull me to my feet. He stepped on my feet and I stepped on his and we laughed so hard I thought I was going to pee my pants. Erika looked over at us.

"You have to count," she said. "*One*, two, three, *one* two three." She made exaggerated movements to help us out. Justin and I continued laughing and I threw my head back in a dramatic gesture.

Erika and Gianni had us beat in the dancing department. When the last notes of the song played, he dipped her low and they ended with a flourish.

"You got rhythm, girl," I said to Erika.

"It's been part of our Best Buddy times," said Gianni. "I have a friend who is a ballroom dance teacher so he taught us."

We wrapped up the meeting and Justin and I headed to my car.

"That was so much fun," I said.

"It was." He put his arm around my shoulder. "Thankfully Erika gave us lessons," he whispered in my ear.

"Ha ha. You got that right. We were a bit of a disaster. I'm looking forward to Thursday." I wrapped my arm around his waist.

"Save me a dance, okay?" He tickled my arm.

"You're on." I snuggled in closer to him.

Thursday morning, I awoke in a panic. What if Harrison decided not to come? What if he wasn't capable of this kind of social interaction yet? What if I blew it with him? What if he wouldn't walk into the room? I wanted him to have a good time. I walked in the kitchen and — surprise, surprise — my mother had not left for work yet.

"What is all that stuff in the fridge?" she asked.

"It's for the party tonight."

"What party?"

I rolled my eyes. "The Best Buddies Halloween party. I've only told you about it a million times."

"You made all that?"

"Yeah. It was fun too. Took me hours."

"I bet it did."

"Go ahead," I said, taking out the container of orange juice from the fridge and admiring my handiwork at the same time. I turned to her. "Say it. I wasted my time."

"I wasn't going to say that, Anna."

"Oh, yes you were. Or you wanted to."

"Why do you always think the worst of me?" She poured her coffee down the sink and put her mug in the dishwasher before she glanced at the clock. "I'd better go. I have a full docket today." As she was leaving the kitchen, she put her hand on my shoulder. "I hope tonight works out the way you want it to."

# CHAPTER SEVENTEEN
## HARRISON

My Cheerios were in my bowl and an unpeeled banana and hardboiled egg sat beside the bowl on a plate. I had the same breakfast every morning. And I liked to peel the banana instead of having it peeled and sliced in my cereal but my mother peeled my egg. Sometimes, my mother tried to get me to eat bacon during the week but I only liked it on Sunday when I had scrambled eggs.

After I'd finished my egg, my mother asked, "Do you have your costume in your backpack?" My mother sat down with her egg. Joel wasn't at the table yet because he didn't like to get out of bed in the morning.

My father looked up from his breakfast, which was also a bowl of Cheerios. Sometimes he ate granola. I didn't like granola because it was too unpredictable, every bowl was different and I didn't like how the amount of raisins changed in every serving. One time I counted all the raisins and it made me late and I had a meltdown. My mother said no more granola.

"It's not a costume," I said. "It's a t-shirt from the Science Centre. I haven't been to the Science Centre in thirteen days." My hands started to flap a little. I didn't want them flapping today, not when I was supposed to go to a dance with Anna.

"Are you okay?" my mom asked me.

"Where will I put it on? I can't change in the change room. What if another boy is in the change room? Or more than one boy? They will laugh at me."

"Joel will help you," said my father. He looked at the clock and shook his head. "Where is he, anyway?"

"I'm here," muttered Joel as he walked into the kitchen. His hair was sticking straight up and his eyes looked as if they were only half open.

"I don't want to dance," I said.

"You don't have to," said my mom. "If you don't want to."

"I don't know how," I said. "What if they square dance? I'm not good at square dancing. We've been doing it in phys ed and I always have to be partners with the boy with bad body odour. What if Anna wears perfume?"

"She won't," said Joel. "I told her you didn't like it." He sat down and poured Cheerios into a bowl.

"I don't want to square dance," I said.

"Dancing isn't hard, Harrison," said my father. He got up from the table. "Watch," he said. "Your mom and I will dance and show you how it should be done."

My mom laughed when my dad pulled her into his arms and started to swirl her around the kitchen.

"Seriously?" Joel groaned. "It's not even eight o'clock in the morning."

"Shouldn't there be music?" I asked. Time was ticking and I couldn't be late for school and the morning was confusing me because my mother and father were dancing in the kitchen.

My dad started whistling and my mother laughed even louder and I didn't like how the morning wasn't going like it normally did.

"Harrison," said my mother, "don't try to be fancy, just move your feet. Watch your dad."

"I can't take this," said Joel. "What is with you two?"

"I don't want to touch someone," I said.

"It's hardly a touch," said my mother.

My mom and dad stopped dancing and my mother came over to me. "You can dance apart if you want. Just tell her that's the way you want to do it. Then just move your feet. It'll be fun."

"I'm leaving in five." Joel stood up. He tipped the cereal bowl to his mouth and slurped down the milk. I didn't like it when he did that.

"Here's your lunch, Harrison," said Mom. "Go up and brush your teeth."

I put my lunch in my backpack and went upstairs to brush my teeth because that was something I did every morning after I ate my egg.

"What if she kisses me like the girl kissed the boy on the television show?" I asked Joel in the car on the way to school. I was sitting in the front and Joel was driving the speed limit.

"She won't kiss you."

"Alan says she might kiss me. Kissing transmits germs. Hepatitis B can be transmitted through an open sore on the mouth and sometimes the sores are hard to see with the naked eye. And saliva is the main cause of mononucleosis."

"Relax. I can guarantee that she is not going to kiss you. She's just your friend. Alan just wants a girl to kiss *him*. That's why he's saying something like that."

"We watched a video on kissing." I glanced at the speedometer. Joel was going the speed limit.

Joel laughed and slapped his steering wheel with his hand. "You guys were watching kissing videos? That is hilarious."

"Yes. It was a step-by-step instructional video on a first kiss. But I don't want to kiss her. hepatitis B —"

"Stop, okay?" He shook his head and pressed on the gas. "Don't worry, Bud. You won't be kissing anyone tonight."

I glanced at the speedometer. "You're driving over the speed limit. Did you know that if you hit someone while driving over the speed limit the impact is —"

Joel pulled the car over to the side of the road. "Get in the back."

Joel met me after school by the flag and I *sort of* wanted to go home and watch *Grey's Anatomy* at 3:30 instead of going to the dance but my mom was taping it, so I *sort of* wanted to see Anna and wear my shirt and go to the Halloween dance. Today it was okay that I wasn't going to go home and watch *Grey's Anatomy* at 3:30 because I could watch it later at 4:30 or even 5:30 or 6:30. But that would be after dinner. The first time I went to the meeting for Best Buddies, forty-two days ago, I watched it at a later time and everything worked out just fine.

"Let's get you changed," Joel said.

I followed him into the change room, but didn't lift my

head and instead stared down at the grey tiles on the floor. There were so many of them and I didn't want to step on the lines. Joel kept stopping for me to catch up to him.

"Forget the lines," he said. "It will be midnight before we get to the dance if you don't hustle a bit."

I hoped no one would see me changing, taking off my shirt, and showing my skin and chest that had hardly any hair yet. Once I had been pushed into the shower by a group of boys when I was in the change room and now I'm only allowed to go in with Joel because my parents went to the school and complained. No one ever hurts me when I'm with Joel because he would fight them and push them back and he's a hockey player and everyone knows he can fight really well. I don't even have to get changed for phys ed.

"You're safe here," he said. "Let me help you."

I nodded. My throat was dry. I couldn't see any feet or hear anyone, so maybe we were alone. I was sweating under my armpits and I hoped I didn't get body odour like the boy I had to dance with in phys ed.

"Is the shirt in your pack?" Joel asked.

I nodded. "Have you kissed Marnie?" I asked.

"Don't start on that again," he said. "Take off the shirt you have on."

I took off my shirt, and a waft of cold air on my bare skin made me shiver. I crossed my arms over my chest.

"Don't worry," Joel said quietly. "No one is around."

I put the shirt on over my head.

"It looks good, Bud." He put my other shirt in my backpack.

"If a girl kisses me and she has an open sore she can give

me hepatitis B or herpes. Or she can give me mononucleosis. Both viral and bacterial infections are spread through saliva."

"Harrison, stop. Go to the dance. Have fun. No one is going to kiss you."

Joel started to walk out of the change room, and I followed, staring at the heels on his running shoes, which were Nike runners.

"I like Anna," I said.

Joel stopped walking and I almost bumped into him. He grabbed me by the shoulders and said, "I'm glad you like her and you're going to this dance but remember: you and Anna are just friends. There will be other girls there too. Maybe some will be your age."

We approached the room and I could hear the music and it wasn't square-dancing music. Anna stood outside the door, waiting for me, dressed in a shirt just like mine with a bone wrapped in her hair but a plastic bone not a real bone. She had asked me if it would be okay to wear a shirt like mine and put a bone in her hair and I thought it was a good idea that we dressed the same since we were Best Buddies. At first she wanted to dress like a cat but I wasn't fond of cats because they are very unpredictable animals.

"Hey, Anna," said Joel. "Nice shirt."

"Thanks." She moved and it looked like she was dancing already but since we were in the hall and not at the dance I didn't think that could be possible.

"He's all dressed and ready to rock and roll," said Joel.

"You look good, Harrison," she said.

"Thank you. So do you. I like your costume." My mother had told me to tell her that I liked her costume.

"Mom's picking you up at 5:30," said Joel. He slapped my back. "But you can also call me to be picked up earlier if you want. Mom has to meet some parents at her school."

"I know," I said.

As soon as Joel had walked away, Anna said, "Let's go in."

I nodded. Getting across the line was hard. Step. Back. Step. Back. Step. Back. Then I had to repeat it all. Three more times.

"You can do it, Harrison," said Anna. I liked that she spoke in a soft tone and didn't push me like Joel did sometimes when he got impatient with me.

After three sets of three, I made it in. And I breathed. Looking around, I saw the food table and I didn't like how the food was mixed and made into funny things, like eyeballs and fingers. Anna had already told me that there would be food like this at the dance so I had been warned, and when I told my mother she said not to look at it so I didn't. I saw another table and there was a plate of carrots and a plate of cauliflower and a plate of broccoli and little individual bowls with pretzels. I like pretzels.

"There's a Lego table," said Anna, pointing to a table that had a bin of Lego. There wasn't as much as what I had at home, and it was basic Lego and not Mind Storm Lego, but there was enough to build a bridge, like Alan and I used to when we were little. A part of me wanted to go over there and start building a bridge but I didn't because I was at a dance. I was supposed to be a teenager and do what teens did.

"I want to dance," I said.

"Okay," said Anna, "let's dance."

The desks had all been moved to the side to make an empty

square. A girl named Erika, who I knew from my English class, was dancing with a boy named Gianni who I didn't really know that well because he was older than me and was not a friend of Joel's. They were the only ones dancing although there were sixteen other people at the dance. The song was fast and Joel said when dancing to a fast song I wouldn't have to touch my partner. I stared down at Anna's feet and tried to move mine the same way but found it really hard so I just moved one foot forward, brought it back, then I moved the other foot the same way, sort of how I moved my feet when I went through a door.

"Good job, Harrison," said Anna.

"Thank you," I replied, knowing I was being appropriate.

The song ended and Anna asked, "Would you like to get a drink?" She pointed to a table with plastic cups and when she did she leaned into me and we touched arms and I wasn't sure if it was by accident. I didn't move away from her and let her touch me and my skin didn't burn and it felt pleasant against my arm, making me feel good about myself and how I was handling the dance and being with Anna. So far, she hadn't tried to kiss me like the girl did to the boy on the television show, so I was relieved and figured that for once, Joel might be right about something.

"Yes, please," I said, answering her question about getting a drink.

We walked over to the table with the drinks and Justin was there, filling up the plastic glasses with orange juice or apple juice or water or punch but I didn't want punch because it was a mixture of drinks. I chose orange juice.

"You did a great job dancing," Justin said to me.

"Thank you," I said.

Anna and Justin didn't touch each other and that was a good thing because she had just touched me and if she touched me again after he had touched her then I would get his germs. I didn't mind Anna's germs because my skin didn't burn when she touched me, but I knew I didn't want Justin's germs.

After our drink, Anna asked me if I wanted to dance again. She said we should try and waltz like Gianni and Erika were doing and some of the other Best Buddies too. More people were dancing now. One girl had tattoos and I didn't want to dance near her so I suggested to Anna that we dance on the other side of the room. Anna held out her arms and put one on my shoulder and one on my waist.

"Is that okay?" she asked.

"Yes," I answered because we were touching where our clothes were and not skin.

Then she told me to put my hand on her shoulder and the other one on her waist and I did and it felt okay too and it wasn't like the teens in the television show because we weren't pressing our bodies together. No one in the room pressed their bodies together because we were waltzing and it was a dance most of us had learned in phys ed class.

"Now, we have to count *one*-two-three," she said.

My feet didn't move very well but Anna didn't mind when I trampled all over her toes and we moved in the one-two-three pattern and since I liked the number three I didn't find it too hard to follow.

"You're doing great, Harrison."

"Thank you," I said.

"Maybe you could dance with Erika next," she said.

"No, thank you," I said. She was dressed like a bunny and

although I didn't have an aversion to bunnies, I didn't want to dance with her because she wasn't my friend yet.

The song ended and we went over to Justin and got another drink and I also ate some pretzels and avoided looking at the table with all the food that was mixed, although a lot of the people at the dance were eating the food on that table, especially Erika. I had to watch Justin and Anna closely to see if they were touching because Anna had touched me and I didn't want his germs if he had been touching her. But they didn't touch.

The music changed and it sounded like square-dancing music. "I'm going to build some Lego," I said to Anna. Square dancing was hard and you had to do too many moves plus the dancing had tired my brain out and I could feel that it was getting filled up with words and noises and I didn't want it to because I was having fun and feeling like a teenager from the television shows. My mother had said to build something with the Lego if I felt overloaded. She said there was nothing wrong with taking a break because being at a dance for an hour and a half which was ninety minutes would be taxing and might make me start spinning. I was also to leave right away if I started spinning and tell Anna to call Joel.

"Okay," said Anna. "I'm proud of you, Harrison. We all need breaks sometimes."

"I'm proud of myself too," I replied.

She laughed and I liked the sound of her voice.

I went to the Lego table and started to build a bridge, just a little one, because I knew I didn't have enough Lego, or enough time, to build a big one because my mother was picking me up at 5:30 and it was already 4:30. Sometimes at home I would build a bridge for over six hours. After working on my bridge for only five minutes, I felt the urge to pee. I had drunk too much liquid and I hadn't gone home yet. Every day, as soon as I got home from school, and before *Grey's Anatomy*, I urinated because I held it in all day unless I was desperate. Then I might sneak outside and go behind a tree. Today I hadn't done that. Why did I have so many drinks? I tried to think of what door I should go out and if there was a tree for me to urinate behind. I knew I couldn't hold it and I couldn't use the restrooms. I snapped on a few more Lego pieces and tried to hold it. I had to go. I glanced at the clock and it was now only 4:31 and I couldn't wait until 5:30.

Since school was over for the day, there would be no students outside, so I could take my hand sanitizer with me and urinate right outside the door. I looked around for Anna and when I couldn't see her I thought maybe she had gone to the restroom too. If she had used the restroom, I wasn't sure if I could dance with her again because she could have picked up germs in there. My hands started to flap thinking of the germs on her hands.

I needed to sit on my hands but I couldn't sit because I had to urinate so badly and I felt as if I might go in my pants. I got up and went to my backpack to get my hand sanitizer but I couldn't find it because Joel had put my other shirt in my bag and it wasn't folded right. The square-dancing music got louder. The voices of people dancing got louder. I had to urinate. I needed my hand sanitizer. I shouldn't have come to the dance. *Grey's Anatomy* would be over by now. I would have gone when I got home, right away. I drank two drinks. I couldn't find it. Where was it? Why did Joel put my shirt in my bag without folding it? The square-dancing music was still playing. Everyone was laughing. Why was the music so loud? I didn't want to dance anymore because I didn't know how to square dance. I wanted to go home and urinate in my own toilet.

I finally found the hand sanitizer and by now there were more people dancing and they were in a line and laughing and square dancing and sometimes with square dancing you changed partners and what if someone had body odour? I had to get out of the room. When I got to the line to go through the door, my hands flapped. Over. Back. Urine dribbled. Over. Back. No. I had to get over the line to get out in the hallway. One more to make three. Over. Back. I ran over the line and raced down the hall to the back door.

As I was approaching it, I heard slurping noises and my urine started to come out even more. I had to get outside. I didn't like the slurping noises.

They got louder and louder. They got caught in my head. And bounced. And bounced and collided with the music from the dance and the laughing.

Suddenly I just stopped walking. They were kissing.

Anna and Justin.

I had just danced with her and she had touched me and she was kissing Justin and his head was moving way more than in the first kiss tutorial video. It looked like he was trying to swallow her and that his tongue was in her mouth. They were sharing saliva. Then I saw saliva on his cheeks.

Now, if we danced she would give me his germs too!

I ran to the back door, pushed it open and when I felt the outside air I ran and ran and ran. Urine was coming out. I held my penis, trying to stop it, and I ran as fast as I could off the school property and down the street before I stopped by a bush.

"Hey, kid, stop peeing on my bushes," yelled a man. He waved his arms and started coming toward me. "I'll call the cops on you. They ought to lock you up in jail and throw away the key!"

Jail! I couldn't go to jail. I ran away from him, doing up my zipper. I saw a bus coming and saw the bus stop and wanted to go home. I could catch a bus because I knew how to do that and I had a bus card in my pocket because I always carried it with me because that's what men did, they carried cards with them.

The bus stopped and I went up the stairs and showed the driver my card.

Then I found a seat and sat on my hands. They flapped underneath me.

"Stop," I whispered. "Stop. Stop. Stop."

And they stopped a bit because I realized I was catching a bus on my own from school. But then they started again when I realized I was going in the opposite direction of my house.

## CHAPTER EIGHTEEN
### ANNA

Everyone was laughing and dancing and the sounds together were like a wonderful orchestra. The party was a huge success. The food I had made was being devoured and Justin was pouring drinks as fast as Harrison could recite bones. I was so proud of Harrison and had already texted a photo of us dancing to Joel, telling him not to worry about picking him up early. I knew his mother was in meetings and had her phone off. Harrison was taking a break from the dancing by immersing himself in the Lego. The square dancing was working for most of the group, although a few like Harrison were taking a break. Of course, Gianni and Erika were still dancing, although they'd switched partners.

Glancing over at Justin, I smiled and gave him the thumbs-up. He motioned for me to come over to him.

"I'm almost out of juice," he said.

I winked at him. "I knew you didn't buy enough," I said, "so I picked some up this morning. The case is in my car."

"Oh great," he said. "I'll go and get it."

I glanced at Harrison. I could see the lines of concentration on his face, the same ones I would often see at the Science

Centre. "I'll go with you," I said. "I could use some fresh air."

"I'll tell Gianni to keep an eye on everything," said Justin. "And Harrison, okay?"

After Justin had spoken to Gianni, we left the room and headed to the back door. Justin put his arm around me. "It's going amazing," he said with an excitement in his voice that I'd never heard before. "You did a great job with the food and music."

"It's awesome!" I danced in the hallway.

He grabbed me by the hands and we pretended to dance, laughing as we made our way down the hallway. Suddenly he stopped and pulled me around a corner, pressing me against the lockers. His body leaned tightly against mine. Just the thought of being in the hallway at school, even though all the students were gone, made me feel like a bit of a bad girl. I liked the feeling. I kissed him back right there in the open. He ran his hands through my hair and I cupped his butt with my hands. He moaned and I writhed under him.

Then, I heard footsteps running away from us. We disentangled, looking at each other, wiping our mouths. "Was someone watching us?" All my bad-girl thoughts came crashing to a halt.

"We better get moving," said Justin.

A door slammed in the distance.

"That sounded like a back door." Justin ran to the main hallway and glanced in the direction of the door.

"Do you see anything?" I asked.

He shook his head. "No. But I definitely heard a slam. Give me your keys," he said. "I'll go get the juice. You go back to the dance and check on everything. We shouldn't both be gone."

"Agreed," I said, tossing him the keys.

The first thing I noticed when I went back in was that Harrison wasn't anywhere in the room. I went right over to Gianni who was laughing with one of the other girls.

"Gianni," I said. "Have you seen Harrison?"

He scanned the room. "He said he had to urinate," he said, using finger quotation marks for the word *urinate*. "He's gone to the restroom."

I nodded, trying to look normal, when inside I was freaking out. He didn't like using restrooms. Would he have gone outside? Was he the one who slammed the door? Then it hit me. What if he saw Justin and me kissing? I wanted to throw up. What had I done?

"Thanks," I said, trying to act calm. "I'm sure he'll be back soon." I didn't know what to do. I didn't want to panic and try and go find him like I did at the Science Centre. That time I'd made him pee on his pants.

The clock ticked and ticked, a minute went by and still no Harrison. After three minutes, Justin returned with the juice. My chest felt as if it was squeezing, like someone had a rubber band around it, making it hard for me to breathe. A feeling of doom settled in the pit of my stomach.

I rushed over to Justin. "Did you see Harrison outside?"

"No," he replied. He put the juice down.

"Harrison left to go to the bathroom and hasn't returned," I whispered.

"Maybe he has to spend some time on the can." He shrugged.

I shook my head. "No," I said. "He doesn't use public restrooms."

Justin frowned. "Could he have left out the back?" By the shake in his voice, I knew he was as scared as I was. "Go find him," he said.

Once I was out of the classroom, I sprinted down the hall, and pushed open the back door that I had heard slam. I scanned the field, looking at the trees, hoping to see him relieving himself. No Harrison. Where would he go?

*Think, Anna, think.*

If he came out this door, he could get around the front from outside. Maybe he went to wait for his mother. That's where she said she would pick him up. I started running and as I rounded a corner, I passed by a bunch of kids playing in the playground.

"Hey, you got a shirt like that other guy," said a little girl. "It's from the Science Centre. I have one too."

I stopped and sped over to her. "Did you see where he went?" I barely got the words out.

The girl nodded and pointed in the direction of the road. "He got on a bus. But that was after he peed in a bush." She covered her mouth and giggled. "A man chased him with a broom and he ran on the bus. The man said he was going to call the cops."

"Thanks," I said. I broke into a run to get to my car. He had to have gone home.

I peeled out of the parking lot, my tires squealing. If I could get there before him I might be able to talk to him before he talked to his parents. Why couldn't I have focused better on him and left Justin alone for one more lousy hour?

I parked by the curb in front of his house at 4:45. I sat in my car and looked out the window to see if there was any movement in the house but couldn't tell. His mother wasn't coming home before picking Harrison up. She would have turned her phone off anyway if she was in a meeting. I knew I should text Joel. He was who I was supposed to contact. But then he'd probably tell his mother, and she was so excited about Harrison's progress. I couldn't handle seeing her disappointment in me.

I dropped my head into my hands. My mother was right. My mother was always right. I had led him on and sent him running away because he'd seen Justin and me kissing. If I could find him in time I could take him back to the school. If he'd even let me.

Maybe he was in the house. Just maybe. I got out of the car and walked to the front door. The first knock was weak and pathetic and no one answered. I sucked in a deep breath and knocked again, louder this time. Still no answer. I tapped my foot and waited a few seconds before I knocked again. When no one answered, I tried the door and it was locked.

Was Harrison still on the bus?

I needed to find the bus stop so I could wait for him to get off.

I went back to my car and slowly drove down his street, looking for the bus stop sign. Harrison had told me he caught the bus to the Science Centre and he said he caught it two blocks from his house. Sure enough, two blocks away was a bus stop. I pulled over to the side of the road. My heart felt as if it weighed a million pounds. A woman walked down the sidewalk and parked herself on the bench by the pole. I turned my car off, got out, and walked across the street.

"Excuse me," I said. "What time does the bus come?"

"In two minutes."

"How often does it run?"

"Every half hour."

I nodded. He would be on this one. I didn't go back to my car and instead waited for the bus, frantically looking up and down the street, the two minutes feeling like two hours. When I saw it coming, I breathed deeply. "Be on it," I whispered. I got out of my car and walked across the street.

The bus screeched to a stop and the doors swung open. I waited. Then the doors shut again and the bus left the curb.

No Harrison.

My throat clogged and the tears prickled behind my eyes. I ran back to my car.

*Think. Think.* Where would he go? I started the car but before I pulled away, I phoned Justin.

"I can't find him," I cried. "He's not at home. He didn't catch the bus home."

"Okay." He blew out some air. "First, you have to calm down," he said, "and think of where he feels comfortable. If this were my sister, I would go to the barn."

"The Science Centre?"

"The bus from the school does go downtown. Give it a try."

"What should I tell his brother? I'm supposed to text him. This is a disaster. His mother is picking him up at 5:30. Justin, it's getting dark out. I'm scared for him."

"Text Joel and just tell him to call you. Then call his mother and leave a message. You have to. Then go to the Science Centre."

"Okay."

The text message was easy. But not the phone call. I

sucked in a deep breath to calm my nerves, hoping my voice wouldn't quiver when I called his mother on her cell. A sense of relief washed over me when she didn't answer.

"Hi, Mrs. Henry," I said. "It's Anna. Could you give me a call?"

I threw my phone on the passenger seat and screeched away from the curb.

Day had turned to night and darkness descended. Streetlights lit the pavement and houses stood bright against the night. Families were probably having dinners together. I pressed my accelerator and drove well over the speed limit.

When I arrived at the Science Centre, I squealed into a parking spot, lurched to a stop and got out, running to the front entrance. I quickly paid and ran through the scanner and up the stairs to the human body section.

"Please, be here. Please be here."

# CHAPTER NINETEEN
## HARRISON

The bus pulled away and I sat down in a single seat, shivering, my hands flapping, and my head exploding. Without my jacket on, my teeth rattled. I sat on my hands and stared at the floor. The bus stopped and started and stopped and started. People got on and off and I stayed on and didn't look up and wished I could walk in a circle. If I couldn't walk on the bus, I would walk in my mind. My thoughts went back and forth and back and forth, swirling and circling inside me. I shouldn't have run away and caught the bus because I'd never caught the bus home from school. But that man said he was going to call the police on me. I didn't know how many stops it was, or how long it would take. I sat on my hands. I had danced with Anna but she had kissed Justin. Had she kissed him before we danced too? That would mean I might have Justin's germs on me. My skin felt like it had bugs crawling on it. Every time the bus stopped, I counted. When I got to eight I wanted to look up, get off, but I couldn't. When the bus started again, I knew I would have to count to eight again.

"Kid, are you all right?" a man behind me asked.

I didn't answer. What if he punched me? Like kids did at

school when I was in the change room by myself? I didn't want to get punched. I kept my head down and breathed. In and out. In and out.

After three sets of eight stops, I looked up and noticed it was dark outside. I got up and walked to the front of the bus.

"I need to go to 237 Canterbury Street," I said.

"Sorry, kid. Wrong direction."

"Where are we now?"

"Next stop is downtown."

"Are we near the Science Centre?"

"We will be at the Science Centre in three stops."

"I will get off there," I said.

"Ring the bell. Let me know. Like everyone does."

Still shivering, I went back to my seat and this time I stared out the window. I knew the Science Centre bus stop. Three was a good number. When I saw it, I rang the bell. I would get off and phone my mother and tell her to come pick me up. The bus stopped and I waited for the doors to open before I stepped off the bus. I knew exactly where to find the phone because I had done this before. I looked down at the sidewalk so I wouldn't step on any lines. Over. Back. Over. Back.

"Harrison!" I heard my name called out. I looked up and squinted to see Anna running toward me.

I felt happy to see her because she was familiar and I was out of my routine. "Hello, Anna," I said.

"I've been worried about you." She sounded out of breath. She touched my arm. I stepped back because I knew she had Justin's germs. She withdrew her hand and I was glad she did. Too much touching could have given me a meltdown.

"I hope you're okay," she said.

201

"Mononucleosis is known as the kissing disease because it is transmitted through saliva. When two people kiss, saliva gets exchanged."

"I'm so sorry, Harrison, if I led you on." Her voice sounded weird, like a bird warbling.

Led on? I was confused. "Horses get led with reins," I said. "They don't get mononucleosis."

"What?"

Because she sounded confused, I quickly looked her in the eyes, like my mother said I was to do, and noticed that she was squishing her eyebrows together like my mother did. I thought I'd better explain.

"You were kissing Justin and sharing saliva which means he gave you his germs and you touched me so I have both your germs. I don't know Justin. I don't want his germs."

"Oh my goodness, Harrison," she said. "That's what made you leave the dance? Germs?"

"Yes," I answered.

She let out a huge breath of air. "Let me give you a ride home."

"My mother is meeting me at the school at 5:30."

"It's almost 5:30 now," she said. "We don't have time to get you back there. I have my car here," she said. "I will text your mom and tell her and drop you off at your house. It's only a fifteen minute drive."

My hands started to flap. Maybe it would be okay. My mother told me that I had to learn how to ride in the car with someone, so perhaps if I didn't watch the road I might be okay. I wished today hadn't been a day where I had to make so many decisions. Everything was coming at me at once.

My head started spinning and I had too much trapped inside of it. I just wanted to go home and watch *Grey's Anatomy*, then eat dinner, and go to my room and maybe build a robot with Alan. I'd missed *Grey's Anatomy* at 3:30. I shouldn't have missed it.

"It will be okay, Harrison," said Anna. "You will be home in fifteen minutes."

The parking lot was empty as I followed her to her car, a little car, and got in the front seat even though I wanted to get in the back seat. I slouched in my seat and stared out the window.

"I'll text your mom. And your brother. I will tell them everything is okay and you will be home soon."

I didn't say anything. My brain was too full and no words would come out of my mouth. I wished I could walk in circles. But I was in a car, and there didn't seem to be enough oxygen. Anna started the car then picked up her phone.

"You shouldn't text in the car," I said. Why did she start her car first? She shouldn't have the car running while texting.

"I'm sending one to your mom," she said. "I won't text when I start driving."

"You turned on the ignition. You shouldn't be on your phone after the car is started."

She put the phone in the console. "I promise I won't text again. I've done both of them now."

My hands started to flap when she put the car in reverse and drove out of the parking lot with just one hand on the wheel. "You should put two hands on the wheel," I said.

"Okay," she replied.

"In the two and ten position."

"Sure," she said.

I stuck my hands under my legs and tried not to look at the speedometer but I knew she was speeding. "You're speeding," I said.

"I'll slow down if that will make you more comfortable."

Her phone buzzed. "Don't pick it up," I said.

"What if it's your mother?"

I shook my head. "You can't use the phone when driving. Stats show that — there's a set of lights coming up in 134 metres. You should start braking now."

I pulled my hands out from under my legs and held onto the dashboard. I couldn't breathe. Suddenly, I didn't want to be in the car with anyone but Joel or my mom or my dad because I didn't have a Nintendo DS in the glove compartment. I wanted to sit in the back with my Nintendo DS. What if Anna got in an accident and I hit the window and cut my face and had to go to the hospital and have a blood transfusion and then I got AIDS? Once, when I was six years old and twenty-three days my mother had been in an accident and I was in the car and I hit my head and had to go to the hospital. After that, I sat in the back seat until I turned fourteen and my mother told me I had to get over the accident and try to sit in the front seat. I'd been trying now for over a year.

"The light is green," she said. "I would brake if the light was yellow."

"It's going to turn yellow!" Then I saw a bicycle ahead of us. The person was wearing a reflective top and I could see the stripes and he was on my side of the road. We had to pass him. I didn't want to pass him. It was dark out. What if the bicycle was red? What if she couldn't see the reflective tape?

"You're going to hit the bicycle!" I yelled as loud as I could. I could hear myself yelling inside my head.

"Harrison, it's okay," said Anna. "I won't hit him."

"No, it's not okay. Stop the car."

"I can't stop now. I'm in traffic."

"Stop the car! Stop the car! Pull over. I have to get out." Spinning. Spinning. Everything in my brain was going around and around.

"I'm trying, Harrison, but I have to find someplace safe to stop, especially in this kind of traffic," she said.

She had to move over. Now. I had to make her stop the car. I had to. I grabbed the wheel and tried to get the car to move over so she could pull over and stop and I could get out. I had to get out and walk in a circle and breathe. I couldn't breathe in the car. There wasn't enough oxygen.

"Harrison! Don't do that!"

Her voice was so loud it hurt the inside of my head and bounced. Yelling hurt my ears. I put my hands to my ears and started screaming. The screams let the noises and words out of my brain and stopped me from hearing the horrible sounds of tires screeching.

I kept screaming. The noise came from my stomach, all the way up to my throat and out of my mouth. I couldn't stop myself from screaming or flailing my arms and legs. I had to get out of the car. What if I hit my head and had to go to the hospital in an ambulance? They would have to put an oxygen mask on me. And put me on a stretcher. I knew I was screaming but I couldn't stop myself. I was too far gone.

Anna pulled over, slammed on the brakes, and grabbed her phone before she opened her door and got out of the car.

Now I was alone in the car. Shaking. Shaking. I sat forward, put my head in my hands and between my knees, and breathed in and out, in and out, in and out. Over and over.

# CHAPTER TWENTY
## ANNA

Harrison was agitated. I pressed on the gas, going a little faster, to get him home quicker. I'd texted his mother and brother, told them I was bringing him home. When my phone buzzed, I looked at Harrison. If I picked it up, I knew he'd freak. He'd already said something about texting while driving. It buzzed again.

"Don't pick it up," he said.

"What if it's your mother?" I desperately wanted to talk to her. Tell her that everything was okay.

He shook his head. "You can't use the phone when driving. Stats show that — there's a set of lights coming up in 134 metres. You should start braking now."

I slowed down. We weren't even halfway to his house yet. I just had to get him home. If I slowed down too much we would have to sit at a red light and I just wanted to get him home and in a comfortable environment.

I sped up a little just to get through the light.

I could see his hands flapping and I knew he was trying to sit on them. Up ahead I saw a fellow riding a bicycle; with his reflective gear he was easy to spot. Apparently, Harrison didn't think so.

"You're going to hit the man on the bike!" he yelled.

"Harrison," I said as softly as I could, "it's okay. I won't hit him."

"No, it's not okay. Stop the car."

"I can't stop in the middle of traffic."

"Stop the car!" he screamed, his voice bouncing off the ceiling of the car. "Stop the car!" I clenched the steering wheel and started shaking like crazy. I just had to keep control of the car and get him home because he was definitely overloaded.

"Pull over!" he yelled. "I have to get out." He was breathing deeply but it sounded as if he was hyperventilating. The closed quarters of the car did nothing to help us and I was also feeling claustrophobic and a huge part of me wanted to cry. I clenched the steering wheel until my knuckles were white. Maybe I should try and pull over for a few seconds.

Traffic was heavy because of the time, and stopping on the side of the road was dangerous. "I'm trying, Harrison, but I have to find someplace safe to stop, especially in this kind of traffic," I said.

Suddenly, he started screaming and screaming and I had no idea what to do. I checked my rear view mirror but couldn't find space to move over. His hands were flapping and he had a scary look in his eyes. I'd seen it before when he had fallen to the floor. He couldn't have a meltdown in my car. There was no room and I was driving. Sobs almost escaped me but I held my focus, trying desperately to get over to the side of the road.

Then he grabbed the wheel, and I was the one screaming. "Harrison! Don't do that!" I yanked the wheel back and missed a car beside me by mere inches. Oh God. I had to get this car over to the side. Harrison started screaming again, yelling at me for yelling at him. Every muscle in my body tensed. Finally, finally, I saw a little break and a widened shoulder so I slid the car over. My heart was racing and my head was ready to explode.

"Wait in the car," I said, barely able to catch my breath.

I got out and cars whizzed by me. My hands were shaking so badly, I dropped my phone on the ground. I picked it up and phoned Justin.

*Answer. Answer.*

By the time he picked up, I was a teary mess. "Justin, I don't know what to do," I cried. "He freaked out in the car and grabbed the wheel and now I'm stopped on the side of the road."

"You have to call his parents," he said.

"Okay. Okay."

"And don't drive with him again."

"I wasn't supposed to," I sobbed. "Mrs. Beddington said I wasn't supposed to. Ohmygod what have I done?"

"Anna, breathe. And get off the phone and call his parents. He's overstimulated."

"Okay." I exhaled. "Okay. I can do this."

Wiping under my nose, I sucked in a deep breath and made the call. This time, Mrs. Henry answered after the first ring.

"Mrs. Henry," I said, my voice trembling, my body quaking.

"Anna? Is everything all right? I got your phone message and texted you back."

"I was driving. Harrison is really upset. He's in my car and I'm stopped at the side of the road."

"Oh dear. Where exactly are you?"

Where was I? I had to think. I had to deal with this. Calm down and deal with it. I scanned the street. "The corner of First and Melville," I said.

"I'll be right there."

"What do I do if he leaves — gets out of the car?"

"Where is he now?"

"Still in the car." I sniffled and immediately after felt embarrassed. I'd blown this big time.

"Go back to the car, and whatever you do, don't start it. Just sit in the car with him. And if you have games on your phone, give it to him and tell him to go in the back seat, play the games, and not look at the road. Tell him I'm on my way."

"Okay. Thank you."

I opened the passenger side door and when he didn't try to close it on me, I said, "Harrison, your mother is on her way to pick you up. I have some games on my phone." I showed him the screen. "You could play them in the back seat."

He didn't answer but he did get out and get into the back seat and I handed him my phone, which, of course, he cleaned with a wipe right away. I leaned against the car, afraid to get back in, in case he jumped out and started running down the road. The cold made me shiver but I didn't move. All I wanted to do was say I was sorry, but I didn't think it would be a good idea to talk to him. Within ten minutes I saw the headlights of his mom's car pulling up behind me.

I opened his door again. "I think your mother is here, Harrison." I kept my tone quiet so I wouldn't agitate him. He didn't look up from my phone.

I walked toward his mother. Was she going to be mad at me for driving him when I wasn't supposed to? This wasn't his fault. I had done the one thing I was told not to do with him.

"I'm so sorry," I said to her. The tears started again even though I tried so hard to make them stop.

She hugged me. "It's okay."

"I wasn't supposed to drive him but he took off from the dance and I found him at the Science Centre. I'm not sure what set him off but I think he saw me with my boyfriend. And, you know…germs."

"Sometimes we don't know exactly what sets him off. It could be any number of things — something you may not even have thought of. I'm glad you found him and that he's okay."

She patted me on the arm and walked toward my car. Opening the door, she leaned into the car and talked to Harrison for a few seconds before he got out. They both came over to me. He handed me my phone.

"Thank you, Anna," said Harrison. "I had a good time at the dance."

I smiled through my tears. "You were a great dancer, Harrison."

"Thank you. So were you."

"Okay, Harrison, we should go home now," said his mother.

"Maybe for our next time together we can go to the Science Centre," said Harrison.

"I'd like that," I said.

I watched Harrison walk with his mother to the car and get into the back seat. Would things have been different tonight if he had sat in the back seat? No. I shook my head. Everything started at the dance. He saw Justin and me kissing and thought he was going to get our germs.

When I got in my car, I sat there for a few seconds, unable to move.

Then I picked up my phone and called Justin.

"You okay?" he asked.

"His mother didn't seem mad at me," I said. "But that could change tomorrow. I wasn't supposed to drive him."

"Anna, it's over for tonight. This won't be his last breakdown. It would be a shame if his parents didn't want him in the program. My sister used to have crying spells all the time and throw herself on the ground. They got less and less as she got older but she still had them. Harrison is learning how to cope. He's made some huge strides in the month you've been with him." He paused for a brief moment. "Are you okay to drive home?"

"Yeah. I'm okay. I'll see you at school tomorrow."

All the way home, I drove the speed limit. Emotionally drained, I groaned when I saw my mother's car in the driveway. Why couldn't she be working late tonight? I'd love to crawl into bed and go to sleep. Now, I'd have to endure her questions. I glanced at myself in the visor mirror, knowing I looked like crap. Here goes nothing, I thought.

I entered the house through the back door.

"Anna," she called out.

"Yeah, it's me." I closed my eyes. I had to act normal, go right to my room, tell her I had a ton of homework. That always worked with her.

"How was your party?" she asked when I walked into the kitchen.

"Good," I replied, without making eye contact. Of course, she would remember tonight of all nights. "I've got a lot of homework."

"Okay," she said.

My back was turned to her when she said, "I'm proud of you."

I stopped walking but still kept my back to her. "For what?" I stared at the floor.

"I had a boy in court today with high-functioning autism," she said. "He got caught breaking and entering because some other kids told him to do it. He wanted friends and those kids were the only ones who would talk to him, but only because they wanted something from him. I think if someone would have tried to help him, like you're helping Harrison, he might have made better choices."

I hung my head. What help had I been tonight?

"You were really good with him the other day in the grocery store. I saw that."

My shoulders started to shake.

"Anna?" she asked. "What's wrong?"

"I failed," I could barely get the words out. My shoulders sagged and my heart ached.

"What did you fail?" I heard her get up.

"Harrison."

"His mother called here tonight," she said, "looking for you. She talked about how good you were for her son. I don't think you failed." She put a hand on my shoulder.

"That was probably before I drove him in my car when I wasn't supposed to. Mom, I made him freak out." I couldn't help but sob.

She pulled me back into her. "If something happened tonight, that's not failing. It's learning. You're both learning. You're going to make a good pediatrician because you care."

"You told me I cared too much." I wiped my eyes.

She patted my back. "I think I have to take that back. You'll learn how to draw your own lines."

She pulled me closer. My back leaned against her torso and it felt good, really good. She stroked my hair.

I exhaled, and allowed myself to shrink into her, loving the feel of her arms around me. When was the last time we'd hugged?

"I think I'm learning too," she said with a sigh. "It is important for you to get out in the real world, instead of just being in the book world." She gave me another squeeze. "We're never too old to learn something new."

I curled further into her. "The real world is a lot harder than the book world," I said.

She kissed the top of my head. "It sure is."

# CHAPTER TWENTY-ONE
## HARRISON

Alan and I walked to the front entrance of the Science Centre from the bus stop and I saw Anna and Justin waiting for us.

"Hey, Harrison," said Justin. "How are you today?"

"I'm fine, thank you. I would like you to meet my friend, Alan." I learned from my new therapist that I was supposed to introduce my friend. I told him I was meeting with my three friends at the Science Centre but Alan had never met Justin and Anna. I've been going to a new therapist, a man, and I sort of like him except he rubs his nose a lot and I don't like that. He is giving me new ways of coping; some I like and some I don't like. I think I should be allowed to give him ways to cope with the nose rubbing so I offered him some hand sanitizer.

"Hi, Alan," said Justin.

"Nice to meet you, Alan," said Anna.

"My mother said it would be appropriate to bring Alan along with us today because we aren't here for a Best Buddy meeting and instead we are having an outing with friends and there is a new Lego display and Alan and I build Lego robots. We are making a video. Alan is my friend from grade two. He has Achondroplasia, a bone growth disorder. We both had disorders that started with the letter A so that was why in grade two I wanted him as my friend. No one really knows what mine is caused from but Alan's is caused by a gene mutation in the FGFR3 gene."

"You didn't have to say *all* of that," said Alan. He shoved his hands in his pockets. "I liked the video part though."

"They should know that there is a reason why you're short," I said.

Justin patted Alan on the back. "A video. Wow, that is cool. Come on, let's go in. I heard you guys are awesome at building Lego robots. And that you belong to the Mind Storm Club. How is it anyway?"

"It's so cool!" said Alan. "All of us just share ideas, so our robot is going to be amazing. We're entering a competition in the spring."

Anna handed me a ticket and Alan a ticket. "I got your tickets already," she said.

"My mother said if you bought my ticket then I should buy you something at the cafeteria," I said.

"Fair enough," said Anna.

"But that I'm to have a hot dog only. No soda. "

Anna laughed. "Okay, I will make sure you don't have a soda."

"But we can only go to the cafeteria after we visit the human body section and the Lego section," I said.

I went in first, and Alan and Justin and Anna followed me. Justin and Anna have never kissed in front of me again nor have they held hands. It would be okay if they held hands because I have a lot of hand sanitizer in my bag at all times.

Joel kissed Marnie on our sofa. I didn't tell my mother this time because I am learning how to cope, and by not telling her about Joel, he is happy with me and he tells me I'm doing great. Maybe one day I will want a girl to kiss me. Joel says I will. But then Joel is not always right. But it can't be Anna because she is not my age and it should be someone my age or at least that is what my mother says. Alan doesn't agree because he thinks a girl in his Mind Storm Club is pretty but she is in the grade above him. But then, Alan is not always right either.

"I have to admit, I'm looking forward to the new Lego section," said Anna.

"I need to visit the bones section first," I said. "It is what I do when I come to the Science Centre."

"That's okay," said Anna. "Are we all game for that?"

Alan shrugged. Justin nodded.

"Good," I said.

Today, I was at the Science Centre with three people instead of just being with Anna by myself. I was already trying something new. If I went to the Lego section first, that would be another change. I didn't want to have a meltdown today.

I decided I wouldn't be using the public restroom today either. That was something else new that I still hadn't tried. But maybe next time, I will.

Or maybe I'll save that for visit number 988. That seems like a good number for trying something new. For today, I just want to cope.

# ACKNOWLEDGEMENTS

I am hugely indebted to the following people for their amazing contributions to this book:

To Tracy Comber for sharing stories about her son with me and for opening my senses to high-functioning autism. Our discussions helped me create Harrison's voice. Seriously. You gave me so much to work with. Pages and pages of notes.

To Meaghan Schulz for giving me such fabulous information about children with autism and for being honest and for sharing all that you have learned over the past few years. You showed me that with a little guidance and outside help, they can cope. You shared your son with me.

To Michelle Eccles for being so candid about your experiences with autism and for making me laugh. You talked about your experiences with love, compassion, and humour, and I appreciated that so much.

To Allie Marchese for working with children with autism and being such a patient and wonderful advocate for their futures. I also sooooo appreciate you reading the book and telling me you will share it with others.

To Natalie Hyde for reading the book in an earlier draft form, and for such honest and sound advice. It was invaluable and helped me make Harrison a richer character. From one author to another, I appreciate your help.

To Andrew Solomon for writing the book *Far from the Tree*. It was an amazing resource.

To the Best Buddies program — because without this program that operates in schools internationally, the idea may never have percolated and become a novel.

To Clockwise Press...thank you, thank you, thank you (three times, to please Harrison!) for believing in this book and this series, and for trusting me enough to make Fragile Bones the first book you publish. Christie Harkin, you worked tirelessly on this book and it is as much your baby as mine. We make a good team!

And Solange Messier, you have been a godsend, giving suggestions and coming up with some last final edits that were missed. Wow. Did you ladies really do this? I admire your literary skills and passion for this business.

To my children, Mandi, Marijean, and Grant, for brainstorming the series with me one morning during a Christmas holiday while still in pajamas. You shared your insights about your high school experiences and gave me so much to think about.

To Bob, my husband, for being my love and biggest supporter.